Rosie Ford was born in Haverfordwest, Pembrokeshire and lived in Whaley Bridge until 1974 before moving to Buxton, Derbyshire. She worked as a Weaver at Goyt Mills until 1969. Married to John, she has four children – three sons and a daughter. When her last son left home to live in London, she started writing children's stories. "Weaver's Knot" is her first novel. Rosie has also written the sequel called "The Moores of Bridgevale".

To Margaret.
With love & very best wishes.

Rosie Ford
xx

Happy reading

THE WEAVER'S KNOT

BY

ROSIE FORD

Published 2005 by arima publishing

www.arimapublishing.com

ISBN 1-84549-016-9

Printed and bound in the United Kingdom

Typeset in Garamond 11/16

arima publishing
ASK House, Northgate Avenue
Bury St Edmunds, Suffolk IP32 6BB
t: (+44) 01284 700321

www.arimapublishing.com

I would like to dedicate this book to the memory of my Mother Mary Ford, who died on the 26th January 1951 aged 39 years.

A wife,
A mother,
A weaver,
My inspiration.

CHAPTER

1

It was five o'clock on a cold wintry morning. Frost glistened on the streets, and a weak, watery moon beamed down on the small cottages where Camy slept in bed. A warm sensation travelled down her back. She woke with a start. "Bloody hell" she said to herself. Little Alex had pissed down her back. She had let him get into her bed last night; he wasn't very well and cried on and off for over and hour. She had to get some sleep, because today was the day she started work. Her belly sank to her knees and she felt sick. Today of all days, she wanted to cry out but daren't. If she woke up the rest of the family, there would be hell to pay.

She fumbled for the candleholder and made her way quietly out of the bedroom, which was filled with the sounds of sleepers muttering and snoring warm and comfy in their beds - not like her; oh no, she had to be the one who got pissed on. Her nightgown was wet and cold and she shivered in the darkness. Camy made her way down the creaking stairs as softly and silently as she could. The stairs door groaned deeply as she pushed it open and she cursed its stupid hinges, standing there in the darkness cold and wet and terrified of the dark as it seemed to close in around her.

Closing the stair door behind her she started across the kitchen and walked in to the dolly tub her mother had put out ready for the Monday washday. "Christ almighty" she roared, then stifled her cry with her free hand. "God my foot - I've broke it for sure." The pain was excruciating and tears welled in her eyes. Camy staggered to where the matches were kept, and thank God there were two in the box. She struck one but she was shaking with the pain so much she dropped it. "Oh no! No, please God, help me!" She'd get a hiding for wasting a match. She knew she couldn't waste the second one. She grasped it firmly and waited for the bright red glow to light up the blackness that surrounded her. There was a scrape, a spitting, and the match was alight.

She lit the candle quickly and held it up to every corner, convinced that the Devil himself was waiting in one of them. He wasn't there. She turned to the sink, taking the washing bowl in one hand and the candle in the other. She walked through to the parlour. The fire was still in, banked up with the peelings from yesterday's potatoes and cabbage leaves, and anything else that could be found that would burn slowly and last for hours. Camy removed the top of the water boiler kept warm by the glowing coals. The tin cup was by the side, and she gently lowered it down into the water which she then poured into the bowl, replacing the top and tin cup. She then made her way back to the kitchen. The green block of washing soap felt gritty and hard, but she was used to it so it was no bother. She took off the soaking nightgown and shivered and shook with morning coldness. With a rock-hard cloth she washed herself down then wiped herself down with a rough towel. In the corner of the kitchen were her clean clothes ready for her first day at the shed. THE SHED.

Again the nausea returned and she doubled up with pain. After a few moments she started to dress; vest, liberty bodice, drawers, stockings held up with elastic (poor woman's garters, Auntie Ada always called them), slip, long woollen skirt, thick linen blouse, and stout strong shoes bought from the jumble sale only two days ago for tuppence. They should have been tuppence halfpenny but Mam had argued with the woman on the shoe stall that they were quite badly worn down at one side, so the old bag had begrudgingly let them go for tuppence, saying, in a low voice for everyone to hear, that she was being robbed letting them go for that much. Mam had marched out of the school room where the jumble sale was held, grinning from ear to ear. She knew she had a bargain for her Camy. Now she could walk to the shed on Monday morning in a pair of shoes rather than her brother's old boots. It didn't matter that they were too big - you could stuff the toes with paper and they would do. Dad hadn't seen them - they had been hidden away from him; he would go made when he found out - when it came down to shoes for the kids or a pint and fags there was no choice.

Camy wondered what the time was. It was pitch black outside now. The moon had gone behind a dark cloud. She went to look at the big old wall clock; the pendulum swinging from side to side was loud in the stillness of the morning. The big had was on 4 and the little had was on 5. "Christ", she thought, "Now how do I work this out?" Her mind went back to school and Mr Roberts trying to help them tell the time. It was futile with most of them, but Camy sometimes got it right when she went over it all carefully. "Well done", said a harassed Mr Roberts, "One out of

45 wasn't bad", when they filed out of the classroom. Later the other boys and girls would mock: "Well done, Camy-knickers, well done". She was used to the 'Camy-knickers' label, she had put up with it for almost all of her 14 years. She couldn't remember when she wasn't called that name. Anyway she went through the time sequence and soon she had worked out that it was indeed twenty minutes past five. She couldn't go back to bed - she was dressed now - so she went and sat by the fireside. There wasn't much warmth coming from the fire so she got a coat from the hallstand and put that over her. She sat back in Dad's chair and tried not to think of the day ahead.

Camy had known she would have to work in the weaving shed when she grew up, she knew it would be hard work. That didn't bother her, it was the harshness of the mill life she didn't care for. Everyone knew you had to work long hours. It was hard on the feet and legs all day standing at the loom. Rushing from one to the other everyone said, and your cloth had to be perfect, or you would be hauled over the coals, sent for and paraded in front of the whole shed, torn off a strip and told to get the bloody job done properly, or you could be down the road. That meant the sack, and if you were following generations of weavers, proud and steadfast, you didn't want that, you would never live down the shame, and getting shot would have been preferable. With all the gory details from all and sundry, the shed was a kind of hell hole, but when you are 'born t' Mill' you have to go. You don't have a choice - if your Dad says "Shed", shed it is.

Camy must have dosed off. She was woken with a start by the sound of footsteps running across the bedroom floor up above her, and Dad's voice raised in anger as usual. Monday morning had begun with a vengeance. Mam was in the kitchen. When Camy walked in from the parlour Sal jumped out of her skin: "What the bloody hell do you think you're playing at!" she cried. "Sorry Mam", said Camy. "Little Alex peed on me this mornin' - wet me through - so I got washed and put me clothes on ready for t'shed." Sal wiped her eyes with the back of her hand. The tears were always there. "Oh well, don't let it happen again - if your Dad gets to know you'll get a good hiding. Get the porridge started."

That meant the big black pan and enough porridge oats to feed the lot of them - brothers Jim, Harry, Teddy, Joe and little Alex, sisters Jean, Mary, herself and little Lizzie. Jim and Harry worked in the Foundry with Dad. Jean and Mary were weavers at the Shed. Mum had lost babies in between Camy and Joe, and she looked upon it as a blessing, although it hadn't stopped the neighbours wagging tongues. "Mrs Moore's having more" - every time she was expecting the clacking would start. "G.. - another mouth to feed - when will they ever stop", said Mrs Jackson at the corner shop to anyone who would listen. "He must be an animal, that Jim Moore. If I were his wife I'd soon put a stop to all that." Her husband shuffled behind the counter and nodded his head. "Yes dear", he said, "It's terrible, it shouldn't be allowed", but secretly he wished he had Sal Moore as his wife - what a looker she had been, still was really; dragged down and threadbare but what a woman, and her having to put up with big Jim - what a bastard wife-beater, child batterer, drunkard, good for nothing waster. She could have had the pick of the town and she threw herself away on him. Some of her friends said she never got over an old love ... she never talked about it so no-one knew for certain.

The porridge was ready. Mam shouted to the rest of the family as they trooped down one by one. Mam dished out the porridge. There was no sugar so they had a spoon of jam and a little milk. Alex toddled down the stairs followed by Teddy and Lizzie. They all sat round the big wooden table and spooned down the porridge. Everyone was tired and no-one felt like going to work but they would rather be dead than say so. Little Alex was still moaning about his ears. Mam said she would put him some olive oil in them and told him to stop blathering on. She had had a rough night with Jim and she hated the world at this time of the morning.

Dad was the last to come down the creaking stairs. Everyone went quiet. There was no talking, just eating, as big Jim Moore surveyed his brood.

"Get to work, you lot - you'd sit all bloody day if she let you. She'd have you soft as shit just like hersen." The eldest lads left the table and reached for their coats, caps and scarves. The didn't argue with Dad - it wasn't worth it, every day he was the same - moody, bad-tempered, belligerent. Most of the children wished him dead; to be rid of him would be heaven, but he was alive so that was that.

Jim and Harry nodded to Mam and slinging their tommy bags over their shoulders they went quickly and quietly. Jean and Mary followed, not daring to ask Mam what they could have for their snap, a bit of bread and marg if they were lucky.

Camy sat and waited for her turn. The first day you didn't start work till half past seven. So she could help Mam dress the younger kids. There came a thunderous roar from the parlour. "Who the bloody hell has been in here!!" screamed Dad, "there's a candle very nigh burnt out in 'ere!" Camy's heart sank. Oh God, no - she had forgotten to put out the candle - he'd kill her now for sure. She started to cry. Mam told him what had happened. "What a friggin' pathetic excuse!" he ranted, "wastin' candle - where we go'nter get another one?!" His hand came down and caught her on the side of her face. She almost fell off her chair. It hurt like bloody hell. She cried louder. The little ones joined in. He hit her again on her back as she stooped. The breath went out of her body. "Shut your bastard mouths," he bellowed at the little ones. They went quiet. They knew, young as they were, when Jim started like this you shut your mouth and looked only at the table. You never looked at him. "Oh, God help you" - Mam tried to calm him down - "Jim", she said, "eat your porridge, you've got to work hard. You need your grub before you go to work." That was enough for him. He picked up the bowl of porridge and threw it at her. "You have it!" he screamed, "you have the fucking grub and shove ... it up ... your ... big fat ARSE."

Mum stood trembling, porridge dripping from her hair and face. Camy daren't look up at her, she just sat and stared at the table. The little ones were beginning to weep softly and whimpered like little puppies. Dad went back into the parlour, got his coat, hat and scarf and left through the front door, banging it almost off the hinges as he left. They all sighed with relief. "I'm sorry, Mam," said Camy, "I didn't mean to let t'candle burn out." "Ne'er mind, lass," said Mam, "A'll try ter cadge one from Aunty Ada when I get t' chance - you'd better be off lass, it's five and twenty past seven." Camy rose with a heavy heart. She pushed her hair back into the large plait at the back of her head. Mam never said good luck or anything when she donned her shawl and left the house. She was busy wiping the porridge from her face and hair.

Camy left the house and walked along the cobbled street. The lamps were lit but didn't give out much light. It was dark and cold - so cold it cut right through to the bone. The sound of clogs on the frosty cobbles rang out, and from every direction someone came hurrying wrapped up against the cold winter winds. Nellie Brown caught up with Camy. "Nar-then, camy, are't ready for it?" "Bloody hell no, Nellie, are't thee?" "NO," said Nellie, "I've had guts ache all night thinkin' abart it, I've bin runnin' t' cludgy for't last hour". The two of them drew closer to the shed and they sighed a deep sigh. Through the swing doors, down the ramp, and into the warm dimly lit corridor. The smell of cotton weft and the warp mixed with a trace of leather with a sprinkling of oil assaulted their nostrils, a smell you only get with a cotton mill, and once experienced never, ever forgotten.

They made their way to the office door and waited with the other lads and girls who stood there. They all knew each other and acknowledged one another. All were nervous. Petrified, really, was nearer the truth. Camy felt a heaviness in her belly. She hadn't been to the lav since she got up at five this morning, and she was dying to go for a pee; too scared to ask anyone, she put it to the back of her mind. The office door opened and out came the boss, Mr Entwistle. He was a stern looking man, big all over, massive feet.

"Right, you lot, follow me!" and they did, in a straggly line, like sheep, white pinched faces turning to red as they walked through the big rubber swing doors into the shed. The noise was ear shattering. What a din - hundreds of looms weaving and clattering away in every direction, with women standing by them. All turned to stare as the gaggle of motley kids trooped by.

Camy hung her head. She felt stupid and uncomfortable. "Bloody hell all that lot of nosy buggers staring at us like was was freaks," she thought. It was cold, too, in the weaving shed and her goose bumps got larger as she walked on. They came to the end of a long wide path, and a woman came forward to greet Mr Entwistle. "Mornin' sur," she said, smiling up at him. "Leave 'em ter me, I'll knock some sense inter 'um." "Righty oh, Jessie, do yer best, yer canna do any more than that," and with that he turned on his heel and walked away. Not another word from him. Man of few words thought Camy, must be summat wrong with 'im. "Right you six, go 'n' standover there to the left!" shouted Jessie. "You others - stay here." Jessie waved her hand and another woman came over. You couldn't hear what they said, it was too noisy. The six moved off. Camy felt her bladder getting worse. "I should've gone t'lav sooner", she thought, but with dad's belting she'd forgotten.

Recalling that, tears sprang up in her eyes and she swallowed hard to stop herself blubbering. Dad always took real pleasure in hurting her. He seemed to hate her - always had - she didn't know why. He didn't like any one of them really, but her least of all. The woman Jessie told the remaining ten of them to take off their shawls or coats and hang them on hooks running round the whole of the wall. This done, they followed the woman in-between the looms. They each stood between two looms looking gormless. For the next hour they learned to change the shuttles that sped from side to side of the looms, to stop the machine to mend a thread. There were a hundred and one things to learn and Camy sighed. "God how can anybody learn all this lot. The woman Jessie moved among them, trying to explain every step.

Camy waited for Jessie to get close to her again. "Mrs," shouted Camy, "Can I go t't'lav please?" Jessie glared at her. "No you bloody well canner, you've only just bloody got 'ere. Get on w'i' yer work, cheeky little bugger. Camy thought she would burst. "Oh, God what am I going to do, the old cow!" she thought. "Serve her right if I piss in the weft tin." She daren't ask again, so she put it to the back of her mind again.

***

Sal Moore had looked up as Camy went through the back door. She wanted to say something to her but couldn't. Here she stood dripping with porridge that bastard Jim had thrown at her. What a friggin' git he was. She hated him and wished him dead. The rotten bastard. She wished him in hell. The little ones stared at her and Joe and Teddy tried not to notice. Eating their breakfast they kept their heads down. "I should have said summat to Camy, I know I should. I should have held her in my arms and kissed her and said 'Do well, my girl'," but any sentiment of any kind stuck in her throat. "Oh no, don't show you care, don't let God know you love someone, for if you do he will take them away from you. She knew that all right. She had learned the hard way. No, no sentiment, no love, no kisses or hugs, just harsh words or a bat round the earhole. She would never love anyone ever again. Scalding tears ran down her face. She brushed them away with a careworn hand, wiped off the porridge and started to wash and dress the little ones, and urged the older lads to get ready for school - it was wash day and lots to be done. She turned out the gas light and opened the curtains. It was still quite dark but the light from the street lamp filtered in enough to see by.

Little Alex had his olive oil in his ears and he started to be less fretful. Lizzie was a good little girl helping Sal all she could, fetching the water from the parlour and filling the dolly tub. Mam made up the fire and soon the clothes were being possed down, then one by one rubbed with the hard green soap. Joe, Teddy and Lizzie went off to school for nine o'clock and Sal sat Alex down with his wooden blocks to play while she mangled the washing through the wringer. The copper had to be lit ready for the whites to be boiled. Sal reached for the matchbox - it was EMPTY. That bloody girl, she'd used both matches, what a waste! She'd get a bleedin' good clout when she came home. She folded a piece of newspaper and lit it from the parlour fire. It went out three times as she ran with it to the copper. At last it was lit and it hissed loudly in the quiet of the morning.

Sal's sister Ada came round with a quarter of tea and some sugar, and they had a pot of tea and Ada had a fag. Little Alex went to sleep and Sal told Ada about the morning's goings-on. "By hell that Camy allers manages to get hersen' a hidin'." "She's a grand lass though, our Sal, she can't help Jim being a friggin' big kid. Cuffing at every excuse. Fancy havin' to start off yer fust day at work after a bloody hidin' from that madman." Ada had no time for Jim Moore and made no bones about it. "The worst day's work you ever did, our Sal, was to marry that shit. " she never went to the house while Jim was at home, which wasn't very often. When he wasn't at work he was in one pub or another, drinking away the money that his family worked hard for or gambling it on nags that never won when the bookie's runner called round. "Can you let me have some matches, Ada?" asked Sal, "I've none and no money till I get the pay packets." That was a bloody lie," thought Ada, "the kids handed their pay packets unopened to Jim and he gave Sal what he thought she should have. "What with the dinner money and everything Monday was a bad day," said Sal. Ada took a box out of her pocket. "Here y'are, Sal, I've more at home. "More of everything," though Ada - everything but kids. When Sal had give birth to the tribe of bloody Israel she, Ada, was unable to have any at all. She would have loved children of her own but it wasn't to be and she had got used to it. Her and Ted, her husband of 28 years, had a comfortable life and they were always there for Sal and her tribe whenever they were needed.

Ada stayed with little Alex when Sal hung out the washing on the lines outside - it wouldn't be much of a drying day but they would be all the better for a bit of fresh air. Then on to the clothes maiden they would go, and be stuck in front of the meagre fire, so you could neither see it nor feel it.

Next came the preparation for the evening meal. Ada had brought round some neck of mutton, so in to the big brown dish they went with onions, carrots, turnip, potatoes and anything else you could find, with stock from a beef cube. It went into the oven at the side of the fire in the black lead grate. It would stay there till about 30 minutes past 6 in the evening. There was rice pudding left over from Sunday so that would do for the boys; the girls were too figure conscious to want any. Sal wondered if Jean and Mary had men friends. Jean wanted to go out a lot lately. Sal just hoped she would be careful and not let Jim get to know. He would go absolutely stark staring mad and she shuddered at the thoughts of it all to come. She hoped he would die, they could have a different life. Lots of men died, mostly good decent sorts. Their women grieved for them. Not me, she thought, I would jump a five-barred gate with bloody joy. Jim Moore was a rotter and a rotter he would stay till his last breath was drawn.

Young Jim had a lass but he never talked about her or fetched her round to meet any of the family. He was too ashamed for anyone to meet his madman of a father, and wouldn't wish any lass to hear the filth that dripped from his father's tongue. Sal shrugged her shoulders - there was nothing she could do, she was terrified of him and daren't answer back. She had suffered abuse at his hands all her married life. Beaten black and blue, knocked from pillar to post. She suffered it all with quiet dignity. She whimpered with pain but never screamed, never let the kids hear what was going on in their bedroom. Outside that room is the rest of the house; whatever he did to her was often in front of the family, she could do nothing about it, only feel dead, mortifying shame. What kind of life was in store for her brood - not a good life, just hard graft and scrimping to eek out an existence. She had only wanted a couple of kids, but Jim had put a stop to those hopes, demanding his marital rights almost every night, punching and kicking her around if she dared to say no. As soon as she had her baby he would be at her again, not giving her time to get over the birth, and within a few weeks she would be expecting again. More often than not, because of the harsh treatment, she would miscarry, only to be at his mercy a few nights later. "Yer my wife and yer'll bloody do as I say. You'll get on yer back anytime I want yer to, right - woman". She would nod her head in submission. "What a bloody life, what a rotten existence, anything would be better than this, and for the umpteenth time she wished for death to release her - either his or hers, either would do.

***

Back at the Shed, Camy was wishing it was time to go home. However, it was only 10 am and round the corner came the ladies with the tea trolley, with toast and marg and a huge urn of tea. "Right," said Jessie, "get your mugs and queue up for tea." The others had a mug apiece but she had none. She'd forgotten, what with the trouble and all, she hadn't got any money so she couldn't have it anyway. However, this was the time to ask if she could go to the lav. This time Jessie said, "Go then - and be quick about it." She pointed to some doors quite a way up the Shed. Camy started off. Women looked her up and down. One or two said something to her but she couldn't hear what they said - the racket was deafening. She opened a door and found herself in a passageway with about six doors, so she opened the first one she came to. She started back, a woman was sat there having a fag. "Sorry, missis," she said. "Should bloody well think so," said the woman, slamming the door in her face, can't have a piss or a bloody fag in peace these days." Camy gently opened the next door. It was empty. "Thank God," she thought, "at last." Her guts were full of boiling hot pittle, she thought she'd never stop. She went right back to work. Jessie was glaring at her, and she ran to her looms, her face as red as fire. Back in place, two minutes later, her sister Jean came down to her with a cup of tea. "Here you are our Camy, bet you haven't got a mug." "Ye're right there, our Jean," she answered gratefully, drinking the tea. It was the best cup she'd ever had, however, getting on with Jessie ... she was just going to say what a cow she was when Jessie came to them. "By gum Jean, is this ere one o' your lot?" "Aye," said Jean, "it's our Camy, she's a good lass, Jessie. I'm sure she'll be na trouble to yer." Jessie's face lit up. She was very fond of Jean and Mary, and if Camy was their sister, well that was all right with her. They had a hard enough life with a father like theirs, without any more heart-ache. She made a mental note to go easy on Camy from that moment on. She was as good as her word. She was fair but firm from then on.

***

It was breaktime at the foundry and Jim and his sons sat down for a hard-earned brew of tea and the snap that Sal had put up for them. Bread and dripping from the Sunday meat. It was good and they savoured every mouthful. They didn't speak much. The dads had little in common with their dad, nor he with them. He wasn't much of a father, at work only when he had a skinful of ale inside him. He was a very different person, interesting, funny, a bit of a comic, a far cry from the Jim everyone else knew and loathed. Young Jim stared at his dad - not eye to eye of course, never that - what a shit he was, rotten to his mum. Poor Sal, who put up with such abuse, rotten to the boys, the girls, to the babies, to all the relations they had who dared to venture round to the house. Why, oh why, was he like this, thought young Jim, they hadn't asked to be born. If he didn't want them why get married and have a family at all, why not stay alone?

His thoughts turned to his lass Tilly. He loved her so much it hurt, but he couldn't take her home to meet his dad. He could imagine what it would be like and his belly ached with hatred for the man. Tilly loved her mam and dad, they were good people, quiet and a bit old-fashioned but honest and true, they made young Jim welcome whenever he called round, but they secretly wished Tilly had chosen someone else. The lad was grand but he was a Moore and that was enough - what sort of life would Tilly have if she were to marry into that family? Mind you, the rest of the family were very nice, a very good-looking lot with good manners, but with a cowed expression on their faces - no wonder with a dad like that. The mother was well liked throughout the town, but she seemed hard and tough, not easy to converse with. They said Jim Moore had women in the town - disgraceful it was. Trollops, everyone said, he probably spent all his money on them, because his own house was very poorly looked after and his kids shabbily dressed, yet with the father, two sons and two daughters working money should be coming in now. Mind you, if it was going to the pub and the bookies runner then you can't have your cake and eat it. Still, young Jim was deep in thought. What was he going to do in the future? He wanted to be with Tilly Bennett for the rest of his life, but with no money and little else the future looked bleak. He had been talking to his younger brother, Harry, and sisters Jean and Mary. They told him to ask Mam if he could have some of his pay-packet to save up for the future, but he knew if he did Mam would be for it from Dad. He was selfish to the bitter end. So what was to be done? A thought came to young Jim's mind. What about Aunty Ada - if he had a word with her she was the only one not afraid of Jim Moore. "Bloody hell I will!" This gave him such hope he sprang up and marched back to work, leaving big Jim and Harry to stare and wonder whatever was up with him.

CHAPTER

2

Big Jim Moore looked up from his snap as young Jim jumped up and sped off back to the job. "Bloody hell, what's up wi' 'im. Probably thinkin' about that lass." Jim had seen him with her when he had been sitting looking through Meg's bedroom window. Meg was soft and cuddly - fat really, but nice with it. He went to her often for comfort after drinking all night in the pubs. He needed someone to laugh with - there was no laughter at his home, just years of misery. He didn't know why he stayed there, what with Sal sullen and moody, never a smile. "Miserable bastard," he thought; he hated yet loved her. Hated her for what she had done to him; his mind went back over twenty years to when he had first seen Sally Smith. What a beauty she was - tall and slim with beautiful long fair hair and eyes that made you go weak at the knees. He's passed her in the street one day. They had looked at each other. She looked sad and looked right through him, while he was smitten. "G ," he thought - his heart skipped a beat. He wanted to shout out loud. He doffed his cap and smiled at her. She turned away without a word. He felt stupid but it wouldn't put him off. He would find out everything about her which he proceeded to do. She was Sally Smith, just back from being in service to some well-off family in London. After four years she had come back lost, alone, heart-broken and silent and she wouldn't tell anyone why. So, her family respected her wishes and left her alone. She was a ghost of her former self. They knew something had gone badly wrong with her life in London. She would tell them when she was ready.

Jim Moore pursued her every chance he got; he was in love with her from that very first day. He would say silly things and act daft trying to make her smile. "Sally," he'd ask, "come out with me." "No, go away," she'd say. This went on for months and Jim was beside himself what to do, how to get her out. He was running out of ideas. He would sit in his room at the Wrights where he lodged night after night racking his brain, wondering what to do. He couldn't give up -he loved her so much he worshipped her, he idolised her, he would lay down his life for her. His every waking moment was filled with thoughts of her. He was twenty years old, all alone in the world. His family had died when he was 12 years old and he had been pushed from pillar to post for years until he had met a man from the Derbyshire mill town of Bridge Vale. There was work in the weaving shed and the foundry for any young man who wanted to earn a decent week's pay. So, here he was and wanted to stay, now with Sally Smith most of all.

There was going to be a barn dance next Saturday night in the church hall. He rehearsed his speech over and over again. He was word perfect, so when he met Sally in the street on the Monday evening after work, he ran up to her and everything came out wrong. "There's a band ance in the church 'all." He stopped, spluttered and went bright red. "I mean, er well - that is ..." Sally felt sorry for him. He was beside himself with embarrassment. "Okay," she said, "I'll come with you." She surprised herself, really, but him even more - he almost cried. He tried to compose himself. "Thanks, Sally," he stammered, "Thanks, you'll have a great time. I'll meet you there about 8 o'clock - all reet?" So it began. He was so worked up he went to the pub and had several pints. He wasn't used to drinking very much so it quickly went to his head. About five and twenty past eight he ventured round to the church hall. The strains of a waltz were clearly heard on the night air. It was hot and he wanted to undo his tie but couldn't yet. Paying for his ticket of entry he went into the hall. There were about 30 couples dancing on the floor and about forty spread about down the sides, sitting or standing drinking lemonade by the looks of it. Jim looked around for Sally. He couldn't see her.. His head swung from side to side desperately seeking her. "She's not here." He was late. She'd gone. Oh no - NO! His mind was in turmoil. He felt someone tugging at his sleeve. He looked down to see a young lass not much over five foot tall; being six foot two himself he towered above her.

"Hello," he said, "How are you?" "Oh, I'm fine, Jim. Nice to see you here. Will you have a dance with me?" Jim didn't want to be rude to the lass. "Sorry, Elsie, I don't dance very well. Will you give me time to get my bearings?" "Right-oh," said Elsie, "See you later on then." She was right put out. Jim Moore was a handsome man, tall, dark, deep blue eyes and most of all lhe was a bachelor. What more could a lass want? She had smelt the beer on his breath. Her family were tee-total and they all said it was a sin to drink. Still, he was handsome and the smell of the beer was somehow sensual.

Jim was still looking round for Sally when her voice echoed behind him. "Hello, Jim. Sorry I'm late. I had a lot to do." "Oh, thank God," said Jim to himself, "thank God she's here."

She was dressed in a blue velvet dress with a high collar and full skirt. Her tiny waist showed off her curves to perfection. Large breasts perfectly formed was Jim's summing up of her figure, his hands ached to hold them and to suck the hard ripe nipples, to be able to kiss those luscious sensual lips - it was almost too much to bear.

He tried to act normal and not really bothered, but it didn't work and Sally slowly got to know how Jim Moore felt about her. "It's not what I want," she thought, "Not now, not ever." "Would you like a drink?" Sally asked Jim. "Thanks, I'll have a glass of sherry if there is any." "Right," said Jim, and he went in search of the same. He was lucky. Not many people approved of drinking but having a glass of sherry was deemed all right. Jim bought one each. What he'd do with his he didn't know, couldn't drink the stuff, no man drank sherry, not a real man anyway.

She had found a couple of seats near the exit doors. As he made his way towards her he noticed she was wearing a beautiful cameo brooch. It glinted of the mirrored globe that turned in the middle of the ceiling. It was very ornate and beautifully figured. The strains of "I dream of Jeanie with the light brown hair" wafted round the hall, and he thought, "This will be our song, it will always remind me of Sally." He caught his breath as he looked at her. "Sally Smith, you are the most beautiful woman I have ever seen!" he said to himself. He passed her drink and sat down beside her. "Bottoms up!" she said, and being so nervous and not really wanting to be here she took a big gulp of the sherry and swallowed hard. They tried to talk together but it was hard going. He gazed at her like a love-sick calf and she wanted to run away as soon as possible. Jim passed over his drink and Sally drank that down also. It was something to do with her hands, at least. They had another sherry but Jim couldn't drink his, so Sally sipped that too. Jim asked her to dance. They did try a few steps, but they were not very able dancers and soon gave it up.

The time had gone so fast, it was 10.30 pm and the last waltz was being played. Elsie came over, obviously peeved because he hadn't had that dance with her, and the way he was ogling Sally Smith was quite outrageous. "How about that dance then, Jim?" "Sorry," said Jim, "Another time, perhaps. I must walk Sally home," and he propelled Sally ahead of him and left Elsie fuming. "What a cheek," she said out loud. The remark was heard by her father. He slapped her face. "Go home, and wash your mouth out with soap and water," he said. She fled mortified, unable to look anyone in the face, and it was all Jim Moore's fault - and she hadn't even danced with him.

Outside in the warm night air Jim held Sally's hand and gently led her down the road. She swayed heavily. She had drunk too much sherry and she was drunk. "How could I. The shame," she thought. "Jim, I can't go home like this. Take me somewhere, please, till I get my head together. This Jim gladly did - anything to have her to himself for a while longer. They wandered down by the canal side and leaned on a low wall. Jim pulled her to him and in the warm darkness, with the sherry inside her and the handsome Jim beside her, she let him kiss her. The scent of roses wafted on the breeze. They smelt beautiful and only made the moment more romantic in Jim's eyes. It was the most wonderful moment of Jim's life. He trembled with excitement and felt himself getting aroused. The kiss went on for longer than Sally really wanted but excitement in her was racing fast. Jer mind went back to London and another time, another place, a warm summer night and a dark handsome man at her side. She was back there. The drink had blotted out all reason and she clung to Jim. Their lips opening slowly, his tongue sucking hers, he pressed her to him and she felt the hardness of his manhood pressing into her groin. "God he is big, he is massive," she thought. He couldn't believe his luck. It was more than he could ever have wished for to hold her like this, to kiss her this way with such passion. He was beyond caring who was about. Their kisses were deeper, more passionate, with such intensity it was unreal. "Oh, my God " thought Jim, "oh God, my I love you Sally," he said, over and over again. "I love you." He felt her hands sliding down to his groin and he almost screamed with ecstasy. He pulled up her skirts and soon he was inside her drawers and stroking her velvet mound. "Oh, God, it was the most wonderful feeling. His fingers moved inside her vulva and he ran them up and down her clitoris. "Love me," she screamed, "love me now, please now." He was too far gone to stop. She wanted him as desperately as he wanted her. He opened his flies and pulled out his large throbbing manhood. He carefully inserted it into her vagina, then he pushed as hard as he could. She squealed with pleasure and pain. "Oh God, it's beautiful!" she cried, his speed increasing. Faster and faster he rode her, deeper and deeper he entered her. "I love you Sally. I love you my darling." His lips met hers again. She bit him hard and he tasted the blood she had drawn. He kissed her deeper and harder and she kissed him back. Her body ached, matching him thrust for thrust. Her eyes were wild. She looked like a madwoman. On and on they rode each other, and at the climax she cried, "Fuck me, I love you my darling William, I love you my darling." She was unaware of what she had said, but to Jim who had just experienced the most wonderful climax of his life it was like being kicked by a mule. He fell to the ground and gasped for breath. She knew his name, why had she cried out "William"? "Oh, my God she thinks I'm someone else."

Tears sprang up in his eyes. "No, no, Sally, I'm not William, I'm Jim, Sally." He shook her hard till her teeth rattled in her head. "I'm Jim, tell me you know who I am!" She began to weep. "I'm sorry Jim, I'm sorry." She smoothed down her clothes. "I'd better go home," she said. Jim sobbed. The woman he loved, who he had just made the most passionate, intense love to, who he had ridden like a wave on the stormiest seas - she thought he was someone labelled William. Who was William? Was he the reason she was always so sad? He pulled himself together and they walked back slowly the way they came, not saying a word. Words would be inadequate at this time. They reached her door and she looked up at him. Her beautiful eyes were brimming with unshed tears. "I'm so very sorry, Jim, it was the drink - I'm not used to it. I don't know what came over me. I'm not that sort of person, really I'm not." Her face was growing scarlet in the gaslight. She felt so ashamed. Never in her life had she been so bitterly ashamed. She'd never be able to look Jim Moore in the face again.

Jim turned and left her without a word. Nothing could be said to ease the pain he was feeling. He had been used, but he swore he would never ever be used again. He would never allow himself the pleasure of loving anything or anyone ever again, as long as he lived. "Damn you, Sally Smith, damn you. You have wrecked my life for ever."

Six weeks Jim worked and slept, existing only by a thread. His mind was tormented and tortured beyond belief. He did his job hardly speaking to a soul. The men wondered what was wrong with him. How could anyone change so much in just two days? They all tried to talk to him, to offer friendship and a shoulder to cry on, but he wanted no-one and nothing. At night he slept fitfully, dreaming of the passion they had shared, aching in every fibre of his being, ejaculating every single night worn out with imagined love-making. What was he going to do - he couldn't go on like this. The solution came a few days later.

When he came out of work one night, Sally was waiting for him. "Can I talk to you please, Jim?" He looked into her eyes, that had helped to hypnotise, bewilder and bemuse him. She was deathly white and the dark circles under her eyes said she hadn't slept much lately either. "You'd better say what you've got to say and go!" said Jim. "I can't tell you here in the street," she cried. "You'd better come back to my digs then," said Jim, and she marched after him down the street and into his room past Mrs Wright, who he had grunted to for the past six or seven weeks. She had wondered if he had gone completely mad; she had told everyone up and down the streets, "Jim's gone mad. He cries at night, shouts in his sleep, doesn't eat properly or speak to anyone - just stays in his room." They had all tried to get him to go out but no - he just shouted them to go away and leave him alone. "There'll be some lass, I'll bet me last gas shillen so I will."

In they marched and into his room they went and his door banged shut.

Mrs Wright was going to shout out, "You know you aren't allowed to have women in your room, you know my rules," but seeing the pair of them in such pain and anguish she just couldn't say a word. It didn't stop her from trying to listen from behind the kitchen door.

"Well," snapped Jim, "What's so urgent that you waited for me at the works door like a bloody wife, wantin' her man's pay before he can spend any on it." "Jim, I know I've hurt your feelings, I'm truly sorry." "Hurt my feelings," he gasped. He nearly choked with rage. "Hurt my feelings - is that what you thought? My God all bloody mighty." "Jim," she chided, "your language. Please, there's no need for that." He gave her a look that almost shrivelled her up inside. "Language," he said - he almost spat it: "Language ... what about 'Fuck me William?' " She cried out, "Oh, God Jim, please, it was the sherry, I didn't know what I was saying. Please don't go on about that, not now, not right now." She looked as if she might faint. "Sit down," he said. He looked at her again. She was wearing a grey coat and shoes and her hair was tied back in a bow. She was beautiful, yet he hated her. She was wearing the cameo brooch again on her lapel. It must have cost a month's wages. How could she sit there, when his life hung in ribbons around him? Her long legs were draped in stockings. His thoughts went to the tops of them again, and his desire for her began to well up inside him. He hated himself for the weakness inside him for having these thoughts of her, after what she had done to him. "What do you want," he said, so loudly that he saw her flinch. "I ... we've ... there's something I have to tell you," she stammered. She couldn't look at him. "Jim - I'm going to have a baby!" When it was said she was overcome with relief. It took all her strength to stay in the chair. She was faint; nausea swept over her again. She clutched at the arm of the chair for support, her knuckles turning white.

Jim stood in disbelief. What had she said ... a baby? "Is it mine?" he croaked. Her face said it all, the look of sheer horror: "How could it be anyone else's?" was written all over it. "What about William?" he said, "Is it his?" She began to weep. He let her. He wanted to throw his arms around her, to kiss that beautiful face, to hold her close and tell her everything would be all right, but he couldn't. His legs were like lead weights. He just stood like a shop-window dummy. "I owe you an explanation," she said when she had composed herself. "I'll tell you everything - but you must never tell anyone, ever. Please promise me this." Jim nodded his head and she began.

CHAPTER

3

They were the Brannigan's. They lived in a large fine house in Camden, Islington. Sally was one of four staff employed to look after the home and welfare of the Brannigan's, Ethel and Ernest, their daughter Ernestine and son William. Ernestine was a lady who's days were spent visiting various friends, playing tennis or croquet, swimming, afternoon Tea Party's, evening dining out at the best places in London and partying the nights away with one beau or another. She was forever in love with her latest and didn't know how she could ever live without them at the time. William however, was quite different conscientious and hard working in the family business, which was a law firm, solicitors and underwriters. William worked long hours always swatting, learning, gathering knowledge wherever possible. He was the junior who could not wait to be the senior partner. It would not take him many years to be on the top rung, then his father would relinquish his crown, so to speak, and leave it to his son.

When Sally set eyes on William for the first time, she though she would die of ecstasy, he was the most handsome man she had ever seen, tall, six foot three, dark curly hair and the most beautiful eyes set in a wonderfully tanned complexion. Square jaw and strong white even teeth. She fell up the stairs dropping her polish and dusters. He looked at her and smiled, she almost gasped for air as she ran up the stairs, ' Oh God, what a handsome man he was'. She said a prayer that night in her small lonely room. ' Please make me beautiful God and let Master William fall in love with me'. She knew she was asking for the impossible, but it was worth a try. William went away for twelve months to France, to learn yet more about the law from some noted French academic. Things went on as usual for everyone at the Brannigan household. Sally had a letter from her only sister, Ada, to tell her that their dad was getting worse with the consumption and had had to go into a Sanatorium in Manchester. It was a long way to travel to see him, so visits were rare, still she and her husband, Ted, would always do their best that she know. However, it didn't stop the tears from falling, thinking of dad, he had always been ill since she was a little girl, her mam dying giving birth to her. So, Ada had always been like a mother to her even though she was only a youngster herself at the time, poor Dad, how could she get to see him. She would have to wait until August 1st when the Brannigan's would be going away on their annual holidays. This year they were off to France and Master William would be returning with them after his year away. Miss Ernestine was going to Egypt with some very dear friends and their family, so she could go home for a week or two and visit dad. She got on with her work, making sure the house was spotless. It was a very beautiful house, elegant, was the correct word. Fine furniture, thick deep pile carpets of the finest quality. Drapes that wouldn't have been out of place in a Kings palace thought Sally. Tables with beautiful turned legs, polished tops, lacquered surfaces, soft glowing lamps and fine china and glassware. Sally loved this house and took great pride in keeping it just so. She had been promoted from junior to senior in a very short time, she had worked hard for this and earned it. She stayed in most of the time and saved her wages of five shillings and six pence per week. Every now and then she went on the tram into London, walking past the Palace, visiting churches and museums, sitting and watching the world go by. It was a far cry from Bridgevale where Sally came from, a small town with cobbled streets, everyone looking hungry, mostly fed up with their lot in life, always grumbling, if it wasn't the weather (it usually rained a lot) it was the price of food, or the long hours at work for a few pounds, the dampness of the little cottages. Consumption was all around, everyone had a pallor, pinched white faces was what she remembered most. London was different, it was leafy in Islington, the air clean and clear. There were huge parks, lots of places for children to play, boating lakes, large dance halls, everything you could wish for. Lots of pubs too, she thought that would suit most of them men folk back in Bridgevale.

In no time at all August 1st was with them and with a great flurry and to-do the Brannigan's set off for their holiday. At last, the house was quiet and the household staff found time to sit and have a drink and a laugh. Cook uncorked a bottle of sherry and they all sat down and had a good old fashioned chin-wag. Everyone agreed that they were happy in their work and that the family were indeed kind and generous to them all. Each one had a tale to tell about one member or other of the family. Sally having downed three glasses of sherry, told them how one look from the handsome Master William had sent her falling up the stairs, not down" Don't ever get ideas above your station madam" said Cook, "always know your place and you won't go far wrong, now heed my words", with that she laughed so hard the fat on her amply body shook like a jelly. She must have been twenty stone, but she was happy with every pound. "It's taken me years to get like this", she would laugh "and its cost my employers a lot of money" at that everyone roared with laughter.

On the 3rd August when everything was ship shape and Bristol fashion, Sally left London for home. A long train journey to Manchester and then another train to Bridgevale. She was tired at the end of a long and uncomfortable day. She didn't wish to see another field or hedgerow for some time. The first sighting of Bridgevale was the smoke stakes with columns of smoke pouring out. It was grey, dark, cold and damp. God, it didn't get any better, her heart sank. Thank God for the clean green London she had grown to love.

Ada was waiting for her at the station. They hugged warmly, Ada was the only person Sally missed in her life. They arrived indoors and Ada was cooking tea. The house was small, but warm, clean and cosy. Sally helped herself to a slab of home-made cake, it was the best she had ever tasted. Supper was in the fireside oven. It was hotpot and the smell of it was driving her crazy. They talked about dad and Ada said she didn't think he would last very much longer. They had a weep and dried their eyes when Ted came home. He didn't want to see two women wailing around the house. Ted greeted Sally warmly "How at lass" he said, in his broad Derbyshire accent . "I'm fine Ted, my you look well, I can see our Ada's starving you to death". They all laughed at his portly figure "Ey ya cud se that" he tittered. "I al'is tell er not to gi me the lions share er al'is does". They sat down to supper and discussed when they would do to see dad, it would be on Saturday morning early, Ted would borrow his bosses van and they would be comfortable in that. Ted was the gardener for old Mr. Squires at the big house and the old man thought the world of Ted and would do anything for him and his Ada. Ted had taken up gardening when he had been injured at sixteen years ago at the foundry. He had been unwell for a couple of years, so hard manual labour was out of the question. Mind you, gardening wasn't easy and Ted worked very hard and earned every penny of his wages. The fresh air did him good after the terrible choking atmosphere inside the Foundry. He was glad to be out of the place and didn't miss it at all.

After a good supper and a chat catching up on the local gossip and putting the world to rights, sally bade Ada and Ted goodnight and went up to bed, it had been a long day. Her old room had not changed a scrap, the counterpane was the same, the walls pale green distemper 'stippled' with a sponge, when she was still at school. It was a small cosy room and she had always been happy here. The large wardrobe still creaked and groaned. When she opened it to hang up her clothes the same dank smell she had always thought distasteful wafted out, Ada said it was woodworm, Ted said it was just old wood worn with age. "now't wrong wi that, last they a bloody life time" he said.

Sally slept well after her long journey and didn't wake up 'til eight o'clock next morning. Heavens above, she was usually up and about for half past five in London, but she had enjoyed the lie-in very much. After a little breakfast with Ada she went for a stroll around the town, bumping into first one and then another of the people she had grown up with. Most of the girls she had grown up with were in the Weaving Shed, so she hoped to see them at the weekend. They worked long hours, dawn to dusk, like herself really, but in a different way. It was nice to see her old neighbours, but noticed how they seems to have aged ten years in the couple of years since she went away to London. It was a hard life in the village, but people seemed to see the lighter side and could laugh at all and everything, mostly themselves. She wandered down to the canal basin and the swans came up to her hissing and flapping their wings. She had always been afraid of them and she turned away. "Bloody horrible sods" she said out loud. "They look so graceful don't they" said a voice, Sally looked round to see it was Henry Perkins, "Hello", she said "how are you?" "Eh! I'm fair to middlin lass. Tha's looking very posh" he laughed. "Not really", said Sally "I'm still the same inside, daft as a bloody brush." She spent sometime talking to Henry and then made her way up into the woods. "Bluebell Woods, she said to herself. Many happy hours had been spent here, sledging down the hills in winter, picking bluebells in the spring, buttercups and daisies in summer and blackberry picking for making jam and pies in the autumn, her mouth began to water at the remembrance of it all. I'd better get back, Ada will have dinner ready. So she meandered through the buttercup fields and smelt the honeysuckle in the hedgerow, it was nice to be here on a sunny day, you didn't seem to get many of them around here.

Ada's cheese and onion pie was waiting on the table on her return, with a dish of mashed potatoes and freshly baked bread with butter. Rich fruit cake was to follow with a cup of tea, it was a feast fit for a king. It was so good, really good to be back in the warm family fold with Ada and Ted. She missed them so when she was in London but she couldn't see herself coming back to Bridgevale to live, not now anyway. They played cards that night and Ted mixed them a shandy lemonade and a pint of best bitter for himself from the Goyt Inn. Old Percy Jennings had sent his regards to Sally and hoped she was 'middlin'. They all settled for an early night agreeing that a good early start in the morning would best suit them. Sally wondered what the day would bring, how would dad look, would she be able to keep her composure, knowing he was reaching the end of his life. He was only thirty eight years old and his life was about to be snuffed out like a candle. He had been ill with his lungs almost all of his life, it was the damp conditions he had lived in. His family had been poor and had suffered greatly, living in sparse accommodation, wet through in the winter months everyone coughing and spitting the day and night. He was the last of the family, all four of his brothers had died of consumption over the years, he was a kind and lovely man and Sally's' heart ached for him.

Well they set off the following morning, it was a glorious day the sky was blue and the night watchman waved to them as he hurried home to his warm bed and hopefully warm wife. The van spluttered and shook it was old but trustworthy. Sally sat in the middle of Ada and Ted there wasn't much room but they laughed all the way. Ted recited poems and dirty ditties with Ada pretending to be shocked. Ted went on about the Prime Minister "What a load of old rubbish he was talking" said Ted, "he wants a boot up his bloody backside" was Ted's way of dealing with him.

Sally liked a ditty more than most. Ted had a postcard, it was of a soldier coming home from the war his wife was on the doorstep waiting to greet him with arms outstretched loaded on a large wheelbarrow was what Ted called his wedding tackle, filling up the barrow. "Look at the size of them, cods struth Ada, Bloody Hell no wonder his misses is looking so pleased. Ada laughed so much she said she was going to pee her pants. Ted had to stop and let her get out and go behind some shrubs, she trotted off then came the sound of an almighty fart. Ted and Sally were is hysterics by the time Ada got back. "Bloody Hell

Ada", said Ted " we thought you'd burst your britches". Ada's' face was bright red but she was laughing herself "When you got to go, you got to go" she said, "Everybody has wind Ted. "I know but there's wind and a bloody monsoon" said Ted, " and that was a monsoon!". They trundled on Ada singing away the song of the year. 'I'm dreaming of Jeannie with the light brown hair'. She had quite a good voice really when she wanted to and the clear voice rang out down the lanes through villages and towns, passing beautiful homes and playing 'I'll have that one and you'll have the next, whether it be palace or pigsty'. They reached their destination, the Sanatorium loomed before them. It looked a bit grim, all red brick and towers, patients beds were on the balcony. "Hope it doesn't rain", said Ted. They found dad in a large open ward, he laid still under the snow white linen sheets, his skin the same colour, God he looked so ill. "Dad" whispered Sally, "Dad, its Sal", he opened his eyes, looked at them in turn, " Ada, Ted, Sal, its good to see thee" he said in a voice so small "How at lass", he smiled at Sally. "Ah, I'm alreet, she said, lapsing into her broad Derbyshire accent, dad wouldn't understand anything else. Ada held his hand, it was thin and wasted, the fingers were like a birds claws and his face as thin as paper. He started to cough, they thought he would choke to death, but after a while he was all right. They spoke about the journey and how things were back in Bridgevale, the weaving shed he had loved so much but had not loved him back. The dust was too much for him, he hacked and coughed from dawn to dusk. "Eh eck lass, tha canna beat smell o shed, its the most pleasant smell as we con find", he was thinking back to when he had met their mother, Mary. She had been a weaver in the mill and they were happy days, he fell asleep, so they left him. Ada went to get a cup of tea, she had packed sandwiches and strong cheese, pickled onions and a nice wedge of pork pie. She took a dozen new laid eggs to the sister for dad. He loved a boiled egg for his breakfast. Sister Hacket said they would go down nicely - in the nurses home later on she thought, no use telling Mrs. Harris her father hardly ate anything anymore anyway, he hadn't long to live. He was kept clean and dry and as warm as possible. It was a sanatorium after all, plenty of Gods' good clean air. Anyway they couldn't get too involved with their patients after all it wouldn't do at all. Remain kind but detached. Ada was happy dad would be having a fresh new laid egg and it would do him the world of good. They went back to bid farewell to dad and with tears in their eyes they hugged and kissed him. "Well, see you soon" they chanted "see you soon". He stared back at them 'Good-bye my loved ones, I'll never see you again, may life be good to you' he said to himself. 'I'll be with Mary soon, my Mary, don't let it be too long, please Lord'. The journey back was uneventful, they were quiet, each having their own private thoughts of dad. no-one felt much like laughter, more like tears.

It was time for Sally to go back to London, where had the days gone, they had sped past. It had been good to be with Ada and Ted , she loved them very much. She said farewell to Bridgevale, wondering when she would return, everywhere she looked was poverty, so many large families, people scuttling to and fro dressed in clogs and shawls, muck etched into the faces and hands of the foundry workers, it wasn't for her, she was meant for far better things.

CHAPTER

4

Back at Fallows End everyone was bustling about, the Brannigan's were coming home today, everything must be ready. Sally was worn out already and it was only two o'clock in the afternoon. The doorbell rang and Kitty went to answer it, it was a telegram for Sally. "For me" said Sally "It can't be, I don't know anyone who sends telegrams". She passed it to Mr Portman, the butler, "Read it for me please Henry, I can't read too well yet ". She was allowed to call him Henry when the family wasn't around, otherwise it was always Mr Portman.

He gave a deep sigh, knowing it could only be bad news. It reads to Miss Sally Smith .' Dad passed away today. Funeral on Monday morning at 9.30 am'. Your dearest sister Mrs. Ada Harris.

Sally slumped onto the sofa, "Oh no, not dad, not so soon, " it had only been a week since she had held his dear face in her hands. Tears came and everyone clucked around her, however, the family were expected any minute, so Sally had to go to her room. There was no time to spend with her, maybe later. She heard the family arrive and wondered what to do, she really should be there to greet them and do her share of the chores. Some time went by and then there was a knock on her door, it was Kitty. "Sal" she said, ready to burst into tears in sympathy for her friend "Madam would like to see you in the drawing room at once". "Right" answered Sally, she followed Kitty down the four flights of stairs, then Kitty went to the kitchen and she carried on to the drawing room.. It was a beautiful room, everything in it was blue. A grand piano stood in the corner to the right of the large coal fire. It was very hot but Mrs. Brannigan was always cold so it had to be lit. "My dear Sally" Mrs. Brannigan came towards her and held out her hands, Sally's' shoulders shook. "My dear, I'm so sorry to hear about your sad news". Mrs. Brannigan was small and plump, very plain like Ernestine, but beautifully dressed and her hair was arranged on top with curls to soften her face, it gave her the look of Helen of Troy. From a distance they sat down and Sally dried her eyes. "Now Sally, about the funeral arrangements, I am throwing a party for some friends we made in France. There is such a lot to do and I can't really spare you. The party is on Tuesday". Mrs. Brannigan was very kind but put her own comforts first. "That's alright madam", murmured Sally, "I don't like funerals, I'd like to remember dad as he was when we went to see him last week. My sister and her husband will see to everything, so I'll write and tell her not to expect me. "That's settled then" said Mrs. Brannigan relieved . "Go and get some tea and have an early night my dear". "Thank you madam" Sally answered and went off down to the kitchen. Cook was aghast, "Bloody Hell", she said "Can't spare you to go to your own dads' funeral" she scoffed "What a poor do!" They all hummed and h'rd and then helped her to write a note to Ada and Ted to explain that she would be thinking of them and sent her love and very best regards. She was glad in a way that she was not able to go to the funeral, remembering dad so ill was bad enough, but seeing his coffin and watching his burial would be hard to take. Best get on with life and put it all behind her, dad had been an invalid for as long as she could remember, she was sure he would be whole now.. He had gone to heaven to be re-united with mam, she could picture them together as they had been when they were young.. Greeting each other with arms outstretched, the lump in her throat got larger and she almost choked with emotion. She put it to the back of her mind, best not to dwell on it.

Ada was hurt and surprised that Sally wasn't coming home for the funeral.. She knew that the big house was very important to Sally and it was her job, but still, not coming, what ever would folk think. Ted said "It's now't to do wi anybody else, the lass has only just got back, she canna keep running back and fro. Anyway she's too young to be grieving, the lass hasn't had a proper life, let her get on wi it as best she can". So it was left to the two of them once more. They buried Sam Smith at the Hillside Cemetery, it was a rainy day and they were all glad to get back into the warmth of Ada's' parlour and make the most of her splendid buffet.

Back at Fallows End Sally was kept too busy to even think about the happenings back home in Bridgevale. "You'd think the bloody King was expected" said Cook "If they start having these kind of do's reg'lar I's off", she snorted. She always said that, she knew they would never let her go, she was their greatest asset. Great cooks were hard to come by and when you found one you hung on to her for dear life.

The party day dawned and everyone was kept busy the whole day and night. Master William was back and Sally couldn't wait to see him. Where is he, she thought, not having seen him since the family's return at the weekend. Kitty bought some news, he's staying with the family of some lady he's met on holiday, Sally's' heart sank, that's it I'll never be anything to him. Later that night he arrived with a young woman, she was very well dressed, but not beautiful, though Sally. He was though, handsomer than ever with the most beautiful tan she had ever seen "Oh god", she felt peculiar all over, hot flushed and quite faint. He looked over at her and winked his eye, she went scarlet. "Jesus Christ Almighty, was that for me", she scuttled out of sight up to her room. Let them have their part, the strains of a Strauss waltz echoed through the house. She danced up the stairs to her little attic room , she skipped around her lonely room and then she began to think of dad and the hot tears began to fall. She sobbed quietly for some time, then she heard a soft knocking on her door, thinking it was Kitty having just finished serving downstairs she called "Come in". She was just wiping away her tears when the door opened and there in the doorway in all his splendour stood Master William. She almost ran, but there was nowhere to run. "I'm awfully sorry, Miss Smith" said he "I just wanted to say how sorry I was to hear about the death of your father", he was ill at ease and flushed from the wine he had had at dinner. "Oh thank you Master William" she stammered, thinking what a right bloody sight I must look. Not to him though, he gazed at her, she was beautiful, her long fair hair was loose, hanging down her back, her large breasts were heaving, her eyes glistened with tears. He sprang forward and caught her in his arms, "Oh Sal, Miss Smith" he stammered and he held her close. "Oh me God" thought Sally "I'm bleeding dreaming". He tilted her chin and gazed into her large deep brown eyes, he felt as if he was drowning "Oh Sally, Sally", he crushed his lips down on to hers, she could only stand there like a lump of wood, what could he do, she wanted to die like this. He prised her lips open and flicked his tongue gently into her hot moist mouth, a thrill ran through her like an electric shock, her knees started to buckle. "William, William " she murmured in between his hot passionate kisses. "William, stop William, please stop or I shall pass out", William let her go with a start, "I'm sorry Sally, so sorry. You're so beautiful I couldn't help myself. I'll go, I'm so sorry, forgive me". "William" she almost screamed "Don't go, stay please don't go". He stayed with her almost all of the night and they fell more deeply in love. He crept away at first light, dreading the though of going back to his own room, wanting to be with Sally for the rest of his life. He knew however, that his parents would never allow him to marry a servant, so what was he to do. He was filled with joy that Sally loved him as much as he loved her but both of them knew they were not to be together, he would see her every night and make some kind of plan for the future, but to enjoy her he would not let anyone else know anything about them. "We will be discrete", he said, "Let no-one know our secret ".

Sally was dressed and going about her duties as normal the party-goers had left a lot of clearing up to-do, so they all got on with it. She had a silly look on her face and a grin as wide as the river Thames. "What's up with her " they asked each other. She was crying for her dad yesterday and grinning like an ally-cat today.

She lived for the nights and for William, she wondered if their passion would turn into lovemaking, she was afraid and didn't know what to do, but she wanted to do it that same night. She waited in her little room, her hair gleaming, dressed in her very best clothes. She had bathed and made herself as presentable as possible. The knock came at the door, she opened it with wild anticipation, it was Kitty, she had wanted to talk to Sally, "Come in Kitty" she said, her heart sank. She left the door open, she couldn't let Kitty see William coming up to her room, that would mean instant dismissal. Kitty went on and on and on and Sally began to yawn, she was very tired, she had had no sleep at all the night before. Kitty looked hard at her, "Oh, I can see I'll get no sympathy from you", she said and made for the door. "I'm sorry Kitty, I'm just so tired, I can't think proper". "Oh well, have a good nights' sleep then and I'll tell you again when you can keep your eyes open". She was gone and Sally waited, her heart thumping in her chest. The hours went by and she couldn't keep[her eyes open any longer. She undressed and got into bed, she was too tired to cry, but her heart ached, he would never hold her again. She drifted into a fitful sleep. Someone was turning her body over in the bed. She thought she was dreaming, a form was lying next to her seeking her lips. An odour of spirits drifted over to her, it was sensual, her mind became clearer, it was William, his lips crushing down on hers, "Sally, Sally", he cried "My darling, I came up earlier but heard Kitty in your room and went away and tried to drown my sorrows. I'm a bit worse for wear" he belched "Sorry". Sally, didn't mind, he was here with her, nothing else mattered. She didn't even think about how wrong it was to have him in her bed, she was beyond all that. She was deeply unashamedly in love with him, she would die for him, "William, my darling", she whispered. "We must be quiet, we don't want anyone to hear us", he said in her ear, then he proceeded to kiss her ears, throat her graceful neck, she thought she would die of pleasure, he claimed her lips and she answered him back kiss after beautiful kiss. Their tongues meeting, touching suggestively. Suddenly he was moving down her body, his lips gently caressing her breasts, her belly, then he was stroking her velvet mound with his mouth, his tongue licking down between her legs. Her body arched and she stifled a scream of the utmost pleasure she had ever known. He parted her legs wider licking and sucking her hot moist vagina, she thought she would die again with the intense pleasure. Nothing could ever be as wonderful as this, shock waves seared up her entire body and she jerked spasm after spasm ripped through her without warning. He then straddled her and she felt a huge hard implement being inserted inside her, she started to scream with pain, what was he doing to her, he was surely trying to cut her open. He covered her mouth with his with such force she couldn't breath, she struggled for freedom. "Quiet Sally, I'm making love to you my darling", he whispered "Love me back, please, love me back".

Making love, so this was it she thought, ignoring the searing pain as he pushed deeper and deeper into her. The pain started to lessen and suddenly intense pleasure replaced it, he pulled her bottom harder towards him and told her to push towards him. Soon they had a rhythm going, they groaned and clung together. She held his giant manhood pushing it up further and further inside her, deeper and deeper until she could take no more. She begged him to stop, "not yet my darling, not yet" he thrust himself again and again deeper inside her, he started to jerk up and down like he was having a fit and his hold on her got stronger. "Ask me to fuck you Sally, beg me to fuck you now". She begged him again and again until he climaxed with such force she was left breathless and limp. He collapsed on top of her groaning and crying softly. "Oh, Sally, my darling, its never been like this before, never", her heart sank wondering how had he done this with before her. She felt so sore but ecstatic going over and over again everything that they had done together. They slept in each others arms for a couple of hours. Then she was awakened by something throbbing on her leg. Before she realised what it was he had turned her over onto her belly and lifting her buttocks he entered her again swiftly and sharply from behind, "I'll give it to you like a dog Sally," he slurred. He was aroused so badly he couldn't speak properly. She bit the sheets on her bed so hard, she thought her teeth would be left there. The pain was overpowering at the same time she knew that he was at the height of pleasure and her love for him grew with every thrust he made up her. He rode her deeply and climaxed heavily. "Next time is for you Sally", he said as he drifted into sleep. Sally lay awake, she couldn't believe all this had happened to her, her heart almost burst with happiness, "Oh, William, my darling, I love you so".

It was five-thirty the next morning when they awoke again. He gazed at her and felt himself getting aroused again. "Come hear, you beautiful creature", he said to her "Let me show you how to enjoy lovemaking to the full." He caressed her, kissed her, sucked and licked her all over until she was like a coiled spring, then he entered her, trusting deeply showing her how to thrust back. They rode on the crest of a wave and shuddered to a complete and fulfilling climax. She didn't want it to end, "More, more, again please William", he smiled, "No more until tonight, my darling", she thought "I'll die waiting , I want it again so much". He crept away and she washed herself down with the jug of cold water left in her room, she washed down below and felt herself hot and swollen and very tender to the touch. So this was the lovemaking she had wondered about. She had heard tales of how everyone said lie back and get it over with. Well she for one couldn't wait to more of the same. Her body shuddered at the thought of more to come. I must be abnormal wanting it again and again, but I do so there is nothing to be done about it. Tonight can't come too soon for me.

Sally waited all night for William, but he didn't turn up. She wept bitter tears but the next morning she was to find out that he had been called away on urgent business. So he wasn't able to tell her about it, she truly hoped this was so. Whilst he has away she got on with her life in the big house and eagerly awaited William's' return. She lay in her bed a week later, it was a hot September night and she was beginning to doze off when her bedroom door opened quietly, she turned as the door groaned to see a dark shape entering the room. "Sally", he spoke her name "it's only me my darling", "Oh William, William " her heart leapt inside her. She held out her arms to him and they embraced, crushing one another until they could hardly breath. He explained his absence and told her that he could be called away any time unexpectedly, so if this happened she wasn't to worry, he would return to her as soon as he possible could. He lit the candle by the bedside and out of his pocket he produced a small package which he gave to Sally. She had hardly ever had a gift, so she was taken aback with excitement and with trembling hands she pulled off the wrapping paper and opened a small box. Inside was a beautiful cameo brooch, it was blue and white with a chain and pin to pin it on to your garment. Sally began to cry, never in all her life had she received such a wonderful gift. William held her close, she was such a dear girl and his love for her grew stronger and stronger. He took her hand and guided it to his crotch where his erection was almost bursting his pants buttons. She opened him wide and began to stroke him tenderly, "Sally" he said hoarsely, "do something for me". "Anything William" she answered, " I know you have never done it before, but you will get to enjoy it as much as I do in time", he held her head and pushed it down towards his powerful erection and before she knew it, it was in her mouth. She started to struggle, she couldn't breath, he held her head tighter pressing it down harder, he coaxed " Breath through your nose Sally, tighten your lips around me and let me do the rest". She didn't want to upset him in any way, so she meekly obeyed. It was awful, "I'm going to choke to death" she though. He rammed it down her throat then when she thought she would pass out he climaxed with such force she bit him hard. The liquid flooded into her mouth and down her throat, he jumped apart from her as she bit him. He squealed in agony. She was so revolted by the taste and smell of the liquid he had pumped into her mouth that she was immediately sick, retching until she could retch no more. All over the bedclothes and night attire. He pulled her to him "Oh, my darling Sally, I'm so sorry. I should have explained to you beforehand what to expect, you will grow to love it, I'm sure, when we have done it a few times". Oh no, not again, never that she couldn't ever do that again even for William. They removed the soiled bed linen and night-dress then he proceeded to caress her all over to lick, squeeze, suck and finger her all over. He sucked her breasts until her nipples were stood out like chapel hat pegs. Then he entered her slowly this time and waited for her to respond, which she did after a short while. It was she who begged for more, "Faster ", she cried "faster, faster, fuck me William", it was the best lovemaking of all and they fell asleep after all the exertion. They continued to carry on like this for some months until that is she awoke one morning and was so sick she fainted. All day long she felt so peculiar, "She must have a bug " said cook" take some Fennins Fever Powder", so she did, but didn't feel any better. When William arrived that night he found her looking pale and wan. "You had better stay in bed a day or two" he said. But she would have none of it. "I'll be alright in the morning", she said.

In the candlelight she could see his silhouette and laughed out loud at it. Vision of his large erect penis, what a sight to see. She soon forgot about her malady as he pulled her over and set heron it. It went deep inside her and she gasped both with pleasure and pain, he lifted her buttocks and then let them down on it. Sally, she was quick to learn the act of lovemaking and began with real gusto, he grasped her breasts and sucked upon them one at a time, while she rode him from above and he had the most almighty climax he had ever known. "Sally, my darling", he cried "I'm never going to leave you, nothing will ever take me away from you". They clung to one another and slept like babes. Sally was sick the next day and every day for weeks, looking pale and thinner. The rest of the staff were watching her closely, what was the matter with the girl she hardly ever left the house. They were all afraid of catching it, whatever it was. Kitty took Sally aside one day and asked her "Are you going to have a baby Sally?. Sally was aghast, "whatever makes you say that !" she cried, at the same time, thinking maybe she's right. She shuddered at the thought. Kitty was sympathetic, "I'm sorry Sally, but I can't always help hearing you in bed at night and you're not on your own are you?" Sally's' large brown eyes filled with tears. " I never thought anyone would hear", she stammered, her face turning bright red. " You had better go and see the doctor". said Kitty. "I can't" said Sally, "If I'm having a baby there will be murder done. "Yes" agreed Kitty, "I don't know what to say, you will have to tell Master William" and with these words she turned in embarrassment and walked away. Sally went about the rest of the day like a zombie and rushed off to her room as soon as she could, there to wait for William.

How could Kitty know it was Master William, they had never even looked at each other when anyone else was around. Perhaps she had sneaked upstairs and listened at the bedroom door. What was to become of her, to have a baby, it would mean instant dismissal from the house, she would be shunned by everyone. Oh, what will Ada and Ted think, I'll have to go into a home. She had heard of girls who had fallen by the wayside and been sent into a home, the baby taken from them. They won't take my William's' baby from me, she wept quietly to herself. She went to see Kitty as soon as they had finished their duties. Kitty didn't really want to talk about it to Sally, she had gone up to Sally's' room one night wondering what the noise was. She had opened the door, they hadn't bothered to lock it. In the candlelight she had observed the young master and Sally completely naked doing things to each other. She had never seen anyone doing before and hoped never to see again, that great big swollen thing he was pushing in and out of her bottom, It was hideous and Sally should feel ashamed of herself for letting him do such things to her. Kitty vowed never to let anyone treat her like that. "What shall I do, Kitty?" asked Sally, "Ey don't ask me" was the reply, "You got yourself into this mess, get yourself out of it". She had heard cook say this many times and thought it always sounded very good. She was feeling uppity and secretly glad Sally was in this state, she was always looking beautiful slim and shapely, while Kitty was big and plain with a large crooked nose, feet like a man and covered from head to foot in freckles. Nobody would want to do that to me anyway she moaned to herself.

Sally could see it was futile trying to talk to Kitty. "Will you do just one thing for me then, Kitty?" Kitty who had been her only friend at the big house. "What is that then?" replied Kitty belligerently, "Will you keep it secret from everybody until I decide what to do?" "Yes" said Kitty "I don't like gossiping, I'll not say anything unless the mistress herself asks me". she said. Sally knew that she could rely on her so with that she went to her own room.

She went over the happening of the whole episode in her mind, over and over again. What will William say when she told him, he wouldn't be very happy about it, but he would stand by her. He loved her more than life, he had said it so many times as they were in the throws of passion. She knew she could rely on him for help. However, William was called away on business and was gone for six weeks, in that time Sally thought that she would die of the sickness, the complete loneliness. Her duties got harder for her to complete but she soldiered on regardless. Her mealtimes were torture, Cook Portman, the butler and the scullery maid would eye her up and down and ask pertinent questions about her health. She would go bright red and stutter and stammer and they would roll their eyes to the heavens. What was the matter with her she used to be such a bright happy lass, full of laughter and always ready for one of Cooks' ribald tales, but not anymore. She was as thin as a bird too, "Never ate owt", said Cook. Mind out it wasn't wasted, Cook would see to that. "Her plate was always full, fat old bugger" thought Sally, "always eating and farting, burping like a man too, she did". Sally could never talk to her she was a gossip and wasn't to be trusted, nor was Portman, pompous old fart. "I wonder if he sees to Cook", mused Sally, that would be a sight to see, thoughts like those made her think of herself and William, "Oh Lord, would they ever do it again", her body ached for him and every night she tossed and turned in her lonely bed, thinking about their lovemaking. She would hold the cameo brooch in her hands all night long, it was like holding him. So it gave her strength, "I'll always keep it next to my heart" she promised herself.

William eventually returned, laden down with gifts for Sally, he sneaked up the stairs top her room, it was midnight and she was awaiting him, she had heard he was returning that day and waited with baited breath. The moment he laid eyes on her she dissolved in a torrent of tears, he held her close, she moved away and locked the door, he wondered why. "Sally, don't cry my darling I'm back I've missed you so I've almost gone mad thinking about you wanting you so badly. We have so much to catch up on, he took her hand and guided it to the front of his trousers, the bulge was already evident before her hand could touch him, she pulled it away. "Sally, whatever is wrong, don't you want it as much as I do, I've got to have you or I will explode", he exclaimed. "William, my dearest darling, please just let me speak for one moment", her body was still raked with sobs. He could see she was very upset so he sat on the edge of the bed and awaited her response. How was she going to tell him, what would he say? She began, "Have you noticed anything different about me William?" He looked at her face, puzzled. "Not my face William", she said "not my face" his eyes swept over her entire body, not knowing what he was looking for his eyes darted back to her belly, it was swollen out quite a bit, it looked odd. Whatever is wrong with your stomach, Sally", he touched it, it was rock hard, whatever could be wrong. Her eyes implored him, " William, I'm going to have our baby". "Baby", he almost screamed aloud, "Baby, you can't, you can't Sally, not a baby, no no no" he collapsed on the bed

His body was stiff with shock. After some time he composed himself, "How far gone are you?" he asked. She replied "I'm not really sure, haven't had a bleed for about five months but I never thought anything. I don't really know very much about babies. William, what are we going to do?" She expected him to comfort her to tell her everything would be alright, but he couldn't, he was desperately worried, he felt sick in his stomach. He loved Sally with all his heart and soul, but he would never be allowed to marry her, he knew he couldn't give her up whatever were they to do.

They spent the nigh huddled together too afraid to make love in case anyone heard them, Sally had told him about Kitty also about the cameo brooch that had kept her going, she had pinned it to her vest. I will never be parted from it she told him, like I hope I shall never be parted from you. He left her the next morning, reassuring her of his deep abiding love for her and told her he would try to work something out. I have to go away again, but don't worry and don't tell anyone about us. He kissed her tenderly and went. She laced up her stays as tightly as she could without feeling too faint and got on with her work.

Things went on in the bid house as before and Sally got larger and heavier, lacing up her stays as tight as she could. William was gone for another six weeks, he returned one morning bright and early, he walked into the drawing room where Sally was alone. "Sally" he whispered softly, she turned, "God, she's so beautiful", thought William. Her eyes lit up at the marvellous sight of him, so handsome he was, he was the most wonderful being in the whole world, she though. "I'm sorry I've been gone so long but I've been getting some money together, we shall need it Sally. I shall come to your room tonight, but I've got things to do first of all. I love you my darling with all my heart. Never, ever forget that." he said. She watched him walk away. She wanted to cry out his name, to hold him in her arms, to love him. She had noticed the dark circles under his eyes set in that handsome face. She knew it would be alright, he would do whatever had to be done. Her baby began to kick very vigorously, but her stays were laced up tight and it wasn't obvious to anyone close by. The day couldn't end quickly enough and she raced upstairs as fast as she could without any supper. She had taken fruit from the kitchen, that would do. She had passed Kitty in the hallway, Kitty turned away from her. She knew Master William was back and glancing down at the pregnant belly she went her way. Sally washed and pampered herself, put on her lovely night-dress that William had bought back that awful night. She had forgotten to thank him, she would do that tonight. She brushed her hair until it gleamed, then pinned on her precious cameo. She lay on her bed aching for William, wanting his lovemaking more than ever in spite of her swollen belly, which was very large when she took off her stays and let it all loose. She though she must be about seven or eight months now, she wasn't sure really, but the fact that she had been so thin beforehand had helped, now she didn't look so bad in her stays. She drifted off to sleep in her wait for William, it had been a long day and she worked very hard. She was awakened by a strange sharp retort, her candle was still lit. William wasn't yet present and she held her cameo and drifted off to sleep again.

Morning came too soon, she awoke all alone and her heart sank. Where was he, perhaps he didn't love her, but of course hadn't they been his last words to her yesterday. I've got to trust him, he will get to see me today, I know he will. She had just left her room as the sound of running feet coming up the stairs came to her ears. She hovered at the top, looking down she saw Norah the scullery maid, she was panting for breath. At that moment Kitty appeared at her bedroom door, "Cook wants you both downstairs right now. Its terrible Master William's shot himself dead last night in his room", Kitty turned quickly to see Sally pass out and fall head first down the narrow steep stairs. They ran to her "Get someone quickly", cried Kitty. Norah stood gawin'. Kitty pushed her hard" get help now you bloody fool" she screamed, and almost pushed her down the next flight of stairs.

Sally awoke , she blinked her eyes "Where am I" she thought to herself, suddenly the realisation dawned on her "no I've been dreaming" she thought. "it was a dream", she tried to sit up in the bed but was unable to do so. She was so weak her body ached in every part. Her head was bandaged around, then she felt at her belly, it was quite flat, she waited for the baby to kick. Nothing happened, she pressed her belly as hard as she could, "Its not there anymore, but it must be, it can't have gone, I haven't given birth to it." She started to cry out and the door opened and the light was turned up. A Nurse came into view, Sally stared at her, "Where am I" she asked.

"You're in hospital Miss Smith" she emphasised the Miss. "Why am I here" Sally asked "where is by baby?" The nurse felt for her pulse, consulted her watch then said, "someone will be in to speak to you directly." With that she was gone. "William" Sally cried out "where are you?"

After a while the door opened again and a mature nurse dressed in very dark blue came into the room, she had a very hard look about her, her steel grey hair was swept back into the nape of her neck, it was very neat but gave her the look of a hooded crow. "Why am I her?" said Sally "and where is my baby?" She began to cry again thinking of William.

"Miss Smith, I am Matron Hackness, you are in a private hospital and I will tell you all the facts as I know them. You were bought here three weeks ago, you had apparently fallen down the stairs at your employees Mr. and Mrs. Brannigan of Fallows End. You have sustained a fractured skull and many bruises to your body. You are very lucky to be alive. Unfortunately your baby was born dead, you were unconscious at the time so would know nothing about the birth". She stopped speaking on hearing the heartrending sob coming from the girl in the bed. She felt nothing for her she was a trollop, Mrs. Brannigan had told her so. "What about Master William?" asked Sally.

"He's died also I'm told, you will have to ask Mrs. Brannigan about it, she is calling to see you today". With that she left the room and Sally was left to weep for her lover and her child.

Ethel Brannigan swept into her room later that day, she gave a look of pure hatred to Sally who lay white and deathlike on the bed. "I will say this to you only one Sally Smith. You betrayed me and my family and we will never forgive you. William shot himself dead because we refused to allow him to marry you, he said he couldn't live without you, the foolish boy said that you were having his child. He'd been sneaking up to your room and you acted like the trollop you are. You thought that you would marry into money, but you were wrong. You have lost us our beloved son and now you have lost your child, all I can say is it was a godsend that he died. We have paid for this room until the end of next week, your possessions have been boxed up and have been sent to your family in Bridgevale. We have told them you have been ill and will be returning home shortly. Do not come back to our home and never dare ask us for money or a reference to get another position. Good day to you". There was a rustle of skirts and she was gone, leaving the door open behind her. Sally lay in a daze, whimpering like a puppy dog. William had killed himself because he couldn't live without her. He needn't have done that, she wept, and the fall had killed their baby, it was a boy Mrs. Brannigan had said. "He" she wept "my son, William." She vowed that day not to love anything or anyone ever again, "If I do" she cried, "God will take them away from me".

CHAPTER

FIVE

This story she related to Jim Moore, he slumped in a chair. "You tart", he sneered, here was he, he had loved her, put her on a pedestal, worshipped her, wanted her madly every night in his bed, had made a child with her, but she was a trollop. He didn't care that she had suffered cruelly through no fault of her own, that she had lost two loved ones. He couldn't see reason, he was blind with a furious rage that almost consumed him. "We will be married as soon as possible". he stated. "No child of mine will be a bastard." So marry they did and a most unhappy marriage there never was. He hated her because he loved her and she didn't love him, she loved a dead man and he took her night after night hating himself for it, always wishing that one night she would hold him in her arms and return his love. The love he never ever showed but felt down to his very core.

So it was that Sally became 'Sal', Sally was too posh for the mill where she wove at the loom alongside the rest of her old friends and neighbours in between babies. The life she had sought outside the mill town now forever out of her grasp. Sometimes she wept bitter tears, always longing for her William. Knowing whatever would happen to her in life she would be reunited with him in death. She looked forward to that day with ever increasing anticipation, the cameo brooch her only memento of her wonderful association was forever kept next to her heart, battered and slightly bent where Jim Moore had hurled it across the room stamping on it and even one night full of drink he had snatched it from her and hurled it on the fire. Luckily the fire was very nearly out and with the cameo being of superb quality it didn't melt, just became a little disfigured. She had sat wringing her hands watching the fire thinking it was gone forever, as soon as Jim staggered his way up the stairs to bed she riddled the grate with the poker and out it came, she made sure he never set eyes on it again. Her little hidey hole came in very useful at night time, but the cameo was always restored to her breast pocket in the daytime, for her alone to know about and to treasure.

Camy's first day was all ups and downs, trying so hard to do everything right she managed to do everything wrong. Her fingers were like thumbs as she snapped cotton threads, dropped shuttles and trapped her hands in the loom. It was a good thing it was so noisy, no one could hear her squawks or bloody hell fires. Dinnertime came and she sat down between the looms, "Jesus Christ" she thought "What a bloody morning" only half the day was gone and she was worn out. "I've got to come here every bloody day, probably for the rest of my life", she didn't want to think about it. "I'll never be able to do it all, its too much, how did everyone else manage it", she looked round and watched the other women go about their work with great timing and dexterity they wove their linen cloth, it was the finest in the country. Women of all ages, shapes and sizes, some with six or eight looms to see to and never a thread out of place. Camy looked down at the hook and metal comb she had been given by Jessie, they might as well have been knitting needles. She was clumsy with them and dropped them into the cloth all the time breaking out more ends. "I'm no bloody good at this", she sighed, her belly was rumbling like a bloody thunder storm. She hadn't eaten since porridge that morning. Jessie shuffled up to her "Aren't ye goin' home for yer dinner" she shouted, although the looms were almost all stopped now it was still noisy. "No Missis" she answered "its washday, mam will be too busy wi that to be makin' any snap", Jessie felt sorry for the girl, "Go and find your Mary an Jean" she pointed to the top end of the shed "they're be up there". "Right oh Missis", said Camy and off she took, she almost ran past the women tidying up their looms. Feeling daft, she came to an abrupt halt "Bleedin' hell, my feet" she said to herself, her too big shoes were beginning to slither about, she pulled one off. She had no skin left on her toes, the other was the same. She staggered on until she spotted Jean and Mary. "We were just about to come down to you Camy. By gum, what's up!" Camy's' face was contorted in agony, "Oh Jean, Mary" she said "my feet are bleedin' with these bloody rotten shoes". They tutted and clucked like two hens getting out the plasters kept in a box which said 'First Aid'. That felt better, Jean brought out a pair of old plimsolls full of holes and handed them to Camy "Take these", she said. Camy put them on and they felt like gloves on her feet, they looked a right sight but she didn't care, she was comfy. Jean handed her a cup of tea, it was very strong without sugar, but she had to drink it, a slice of bread and margarine too, by hell she needed this. She looked up at Jean and Mary they were angels she thought, angels. Her eyes filled with tears,

"I don't think I'll ever be able to do this weavin'", she sobbed. "Its too bloody hard." They hugged her in turn, "You will Camy, you will, we were like you at first, frightened and clumsy, but it just comes to you one day, you just get it all right and then its plain sailin' from then on. You'll end up the best weaver in't shed." Camy dried her tears and laughed with them. Dad gave me a bloody 'iddin this mornin", she said. Their eyes flashed at each other, "why" they echoed, "what did you do." "I left the candle burnin in't parlour", she answered. "Oh, our Camy, you are daft givin' him an excuse t belt yer. He don't need any excuse to lash out, so be careful." Hatred for their father, Jim Moore was evident in their eyes. Both of them could hardly wait to get away from home but leaving mam would be hard.

A whistle sounded and Camy was told to hurry back to her loom. Off she went in her holey plimsolls walking on air, the large brown shoes tucked under her arm, wrapped up in brown paper and tied together with string. The afternoon wasn't quite as bad apart from the fact that she hadn't bothered to go to the lav and her belly was giving her jip again. Jessie let her go with a scowl and she ran like a mad March hare to the lav and back. At half past five the whistle sounded again, it was home time and everyone scuttled off home. Clogs clattering on the cobbled streets, it was dark and Camy thought "I haven't seen daylight at all today." Mrs. Miller asked her how she had got on, "Oh, not too bad, its very hard but I think I'll get used to it soon", she said hoping this would be true "Eh, by gum lass, if yer owt like rest of family yer'll do aw rite." Camy felt pleased at this, yes her family were known for their being good weavers, so she couldn't let them down. Nellie Brown caught up with her before she turned down her street. "Eh up Cam how yer got on?" "Oh, can't grumble" she answered "How about you? "Well I'm fair to middlin", said Nellie. "I'll never do it, I really won't, I'm fed up wi it already, I don't fancy goin back in mornin', but me mam and Dad will make me," she looked angry and fed up. Camy could only agree that it was indeed damned hard work. "I'll have to keep going anyway, dad will skin me alive if I don't keep the job." I don't have a dad like Jim Moore, thought Nellie, so it won't be so bad for me. "See yer in mornin'." said Nellie. "Aye, alreet see yer." said Camy.

The house was full of steam from the washing of clothes drying round the fire and the pans bubbling on the stove, "Hi yer mam", called Camy rushing to little Alex and scooping him up for a big hug and kiss. He was pleased to see her, "Cam, Cam where have you been, I missed you", she hugged him close, mam never seemed to hug him close, mam never seemed to hug him, never seemed to hug anyone of them anyway. Alex was the baby after all, the last we all hope, thought Camy. "You little bugger you pee'd down me back lass night", said Camy, he laughed. "Camy" shouted mam from the parlour "see to them spuds", "Righto", she shouted back lifting the lids. Spuds in one pan and neck of mutton with onion, carrot, turnip and some lentils and barley. It smelt good, her belly was ready for it. She suddenly remembered the shoes, quick as a flash she changed into the brown ones and hid the plimsolls in her coat pockets. Sal came through to the kitchen, "You'd better sort out plates and dish up", she snapped. Her back was playing up again and she was in no mood for buggering about. She didn't ask Camy how she had got on at the shed. She didn't bother, she was too tired, fed up with the whole lot of them. Camy dished up the dinner, large plates for the men folk and smaller ones for Jean, Mary and herself with bowls for the younger ones. The table was large enough for them all to get round it with a bit of a squeeze. She cut thick slices of aunty Ada's' fresh bread and stacked it on a plate in the middle of the table.

The back door opened and big Jim, followed by young Jim and Harry came in with Jean and Mary behind them. The men folk washed themselves down in the kitchen sink before dinner. Joe and Teddy were called from upstairs and Lizzie rushed in from aunty Ada's', out of breath and frightened of the dark. They all took off their coats, hats and scarves and sat down to the main meal of the day. Camy helped the young ones with their bibs and sat down keeping her gaze away from her dad who was glowering at the lot of them. "How was yer first day at work our Camy?" asked young Jim. She was about to answer but was interrupted by big Jim, "Work her, you've got ter bay joking, she doesn't know the meanin' of the bloody word. Stupid little git she is", he said remembering the candle that morning. "She won't last two bloody minutes", he barked. At this she shut her mouth tight and said now't, but hot tears stung her eyes. "Here we bloody well go agin" shouted Jim "The bleedin water works agin" he snarled. Sal looked from her husband to Camy, here we go again, she thought, these two. "Come on Jim, lass is trying her best", she said, a rare thing it was for her to back any one of them up. "What the bloody hell do you know about anything", he barked. "She's a bloody idiot like you, he said, " Christ almighty, Cameo", he laughed, "you named her after a fucking brooch", he slung the dinner plate to one side and kicked his chair, it hit the wall with a crash. Little Alex began to whimper and everyone was frightened to what would happen next. Young Jim and Harry would have loved to beat him senseless, but they both knew he was a bloody madman and not to be tangled with. They were no match for him yet, but one day. Big Jim reached for his coat and hat and slammed out of the house, everyone sighed with relief. Thank God, he would be off to the pub now for the night.

They all started to talk at once and even laugh together after a while. Camy told them about the woman in lavy, "There she was with her draws round her ankles and a fag in her gob" she mocked "yer can't have a bloody piss in peace" she mimicked. "I don't think I'll ever get used to it", she sighed. " Course you will", they all chimed, "you'll do it OK, just give yourself time."

They cleared the table, it was Jim and Mary's' turn to wash and dry to-night, so the others could do homework and such. Camy always helped the young ones as best she could. She had always hated homework herself so didn't mind giving a helping hand. Sal told her to make herself a bit of snap for work in't mornin and gave her one of the old cracked mugs to take to work for her tea break. "There's a penny on the mantelpiece for yer brew take it now before yer dad sees it", she snapped. Camy was tired and wanted to get to bed but there was some ironing to be done, she put the iron onto the fire and got out the ironing cloth and set it up on the table. Grasping the hot iron with a cloth, she spat on it and the spittle sizzled and vanished off the flat of the iron. There was the biggest pile of ironing she had seen for ages, "I'm not doin' all this bloody lot", she thought and slogged away for two hours, by then little Alex was tired and wanted to go to bed, he wouldn't do without Camy, so off she went with him, Mam taking over the ironing.

Camy staggered up the steep stairs, Alex was getting heavier and was a dead weight, her back and legs were aching after the long day and she hoped Alex would go to sleep right away, which he did. so she crept to her own bed, stripped, put on a clean nightie and slid between the sheets. Her mind wouldn't let her sleep, it kept going over all the events of the day. She thought she'd never get to sleep. She heard Jean and Mary go to bed and Lizzie and Teddy and thinking she had never closed her eyes all night, she was suddenly shaken awake. "Come on, Camy", said Lizzie, "everyone's downstairs." "What the hell" Camy thought "I haven't bin to sleep, I'm tired out I must be dreaming." She looked round the room and the other beds were empty apart from Alex's'. She jumped out of bed and dressed as fast as she could, rushed downstairs. The men had just left, which was a good thing for Jim was all for 'draggin the idol little bastard out of her bed.' "Sorry mam," she said "I must have overlaid", "eat yer porridge", said mam. Jean and Mary were getting their coats on, "you have to be there at same time as us now, don't forget Cam." "Oh no" she put on her coat shovelled the last mouthful of porridge in, grabbed her snap and mug and followed them out of the door. She looked back at Sal, there was no wave of good-bye, no cheerio, she just turned away and got on with her jobs.

"Another bloody day", thought Camy "hope its better than yesterday." She hadn't been at work more than an hour when a leather strap broke on the loom, "right Camy" said Jessie "go down to the bottom of the shed, right down there", pointing to a long wide aisle, "at the bottom are big double rubber doors, go through them and keep on till you come to another room with a door with glass pane in't middle. Knock on't door and ask for Fred Wright, tell im belts snapped and Jessie sent yer. Now hurry up and get back as quick as yer can, no dawdlin." Camy started down the shed, everybody eyed her up and down, noting her shabby clothes and holed plimsolls, she didn't care, she felt very important. Anyway, it was a rest from sloggin over looms. She went through the big doors and suddenly there was a wall of silence, it was eerie and spooky, a bit gloomy although she could see daylight far off, up the passageway through yet another door. Having found the room, she knocked on the wooden door, noting the plaque over the lintel saying "Abandon hope all ye who enter here." She read it over and over again not understanding what it meant. Funny thing to have, she mused. "Come in" said a voice, she turned the handle and pushed open the door. The room was dimly lit and she couldn't see anyone, she stood looking simple "Hello!" she said "anybody there" from round the door just behind her a man sprang into view. She shot forward and almost shouted out with fright. He started to laugh "gave yer a fright did I eh, go in", he said "lets have a look at ye." She stepped further inside the strange room. "Who'd yer want?" he asked "Oh, I'm, lookin fer Fred Wright" she said. "An who wants 'im" he asked. She was beginning to feel uncomfortable, she didn't like the way he was looking at her. "Jessie wants him, straps broken" she stammered going red as beetroot under his leering gaze. "Oh, and who are you when yer at 'om?" he asked. "I'm Camy Moore, Mister", she answered. "I started yesterday." "You can start with me anytime lass." he said, licking his big fat ugly lips, he continued to stare her up and down, gazing at her bosom. She wanted to get out of the room, she tried to edge past him, "I'd better get back or Jessie will be reet mad", she said. "Can yer tell me where Fred Wright will be?" "I'm Fred Wright", he answered, "you've found me, isn't that nice now? You are a pretty girl, sister to Jean and Mary he, by gum them two are right gradley." She edged closer to the door and he held her tightly against him pressing his groin into her belly. Something big and hard was beating against her, his breath was evil and she thought she would be sick, she almost retched. She didn't want to get on the wrong side of him but she didn't want to encourage him either, she racked her brain wondering what to do. "Play yer cards right lass and we can be good pals, know what I mean?" he leered, showing dirty brown stained teeth. "You won't go far wrong with Fred Wright as yer mate." He held her tighter and she knew now he was aroused, she had been witness to this type of thing with the big lads at school but never with a man. She started to panic and struggled to get free. "I'd better get back" she began "or else I'll be for it", he was just about to feel her breasts when the door opened and a man entered. He let her go as quick as a flash, "right lass", he said "go on, bugger off, I'll be there when I've finished t'other job." The other man looked from one to the other of the pair. She looked petrified and fled like a rat up a drainpipe. Gilbert Holmes looked long and hard at Fred Wright. "By eck Fred, you're going to get into serious trouble one of these days, you should bloody well leave young lasses alone afore yer cops it." "Just my bit of fun Bert, dunna fret, I'm, harmless yer know that. I wouldna hurt a fly." Bert wasn't convinced he'd seen the disgusting bulge in Fred's' trousers. "What a bloody dirty bugger he was", thought Bert, "Something should be done about im before he went too far."

Camy fled from the room and through the double doors into the weaving shed. She felt safe now, but her heart was nearly jumping out of her chest and her face must be as red as fire. Jessie eyed her up, "what's up wi thee" she said "nothin Missus", Camy replied, "just ran back that's all, I'm out of breath." "That's the last bloody time I go there" she said to herself "never again will that dirty bastard get a hold of me." The smell of him lingered on in her mind. What a pig, she had better tell Mary and Jean about it. What will they say, she wondered. Surely they can't like someone like him. A while later he arrived to replace the strap, he looked right through her as if she wasn't there. He sidled up to Jessie who went bright red and they gazed into one another's eyes, bloody hell, thought Camy, they fancy one another. Jessie went down in her estimation from then on. He stroked her buttocks and breasts when he thought no one was looking and Jessie was like a little girl with a fit of the giggles. Well, well, bloody good job she hadn't told Jessie what he had tried to do to her. Well he wouldn't be trying it again, so that was alreet, let Jessie get on with it.

It was break time and she went to get her well deserved mug of tea. I'll have a new mug one day, she said to herself looking at the chips and cracks in hers. Most of the women had large white mugs, someone said you could buy them from the canteen. She would save up for one. She sat with her tea trying not to look at Fred and Jessie's' antics. She watched him mouth to her "Come down at three", Jessie nodded quickly and turned away. Camy wondered what he meant, anyway at three o'clock in the afternoon Jessie walked down the shed the way Camy had gone in the morning. She was gone about fifteen minutes and hurried back all flustered. Camy noticed her skirt was twisted round her legs like she had hitched it up and it was covered in creases. Bloody hell, thought Camy, I wonder if they've been at it. She knew what 'at it' meant, although she had never been 'at it' with anyone. She was a good girl and wasn't going to waste herself on anyone, only the man she loved and who she would marry.

She began to sing to herself "The Holly and the Ivy, when they are both full grown," nobody could hear her she wasn't bothered anyway. It would soon be Christmas day. Some of the womenfolk were putting decorations around their looms, it was getting quite festive. She was happier today, casting the thoughts of the morning from her mind. The day dragged on, there was the weft to sort out, which weft was used for which loom. Most of the looms using different weft, then you had to put out the correct tins for the weft carrier to collect, making sure had weft for every loom and did not run out, or ' woe betide yer.' She was still learning how to use the reed hook and how to make a new yell if one broke on the frame. Then to top it all as if that wasn't enough she had to learn how to unweave when cloth was damaged, the penalty was sixpence for work to be unwoven and for any damaged cloth. The metal comb she had been given was used for this the process was long and tedious. Women were employed to help the weaver to do this job, the number of the loom was written on a board with the nature of the job alongside, e.g. Trap or Float Trap for when the shuttle bearing the weft shot through the threads and snapped them in half, they then had to be repaired using what was known as the weavers knot. A special knot that if tied correctly would hold like a vice. The float was where the weft was lifted over or under the warp the wrong way, so that you could slide your finger into it like a pocket. It stood out like a huge blemish on the cloth. It had to be undone and made to look like it had never happened in the first place. If the damage to the cloth was severe or ripped, the Boss, Mr. Entwhistle had to be fetched from his office or wherever he was at the time. Everyone at the mill knew that so and so had done whatever, and she couldn't have been doing her job properly of course. So the Boss gave whoever a good ear bashing and was told not to let it happen again. After all she only had six to eight looms to look after and probably five or six kids to feed and cloth and worry about, how was she going to do it. So really all in all she must have been a really bad worker.

To this Camy thought what a rotten stinking job, treated like bloody shit. Always the men giving out the orders too. They won't give me the shit treatment when I've learned this job, she said to herself. I'll be the best weaver this shed has every seen, if I live long enough, thinking of the hard task ahead. She went to see Jean and Mary at dinner break. Mary was alone, "where's our Jean" Camy asked, "don't let on Camy, she's gone over to see that led she fancies in't warehouse", Oh, isn't that Arthur Bennett, you know, Tilly's brother" , "Oh yes", answered Camy. "Tilly was seeing their Jim, right oh, I won't say a word", what would dad say to that bloody old fart", she laughed to herself. "We'll have a double wedding eh Mary", "Eh up now Camy, done say things like that for gods sake if dad finds out we'll be skinned alive, he'd have a bloody heart attack." They looked at each other and burst out laughing at the thought of big Jim dying of a heart attack

"What a bloody relief that would be. We can always live in hope", said Mary.

She told Mary about Fred Wright and Mary told her to keep away from him, "He's sex mad", she whispered, "don't ever be on your own with him, they do say he has about five women here in't mill, dirty buggers. They must be to have anything to do with that filthy sod." They had a good titter, then Camy went back to her work. She waved to Jean who was just coming back from the warehouse looking flushed and pretty, "must be in love", thought Camy.

On the way home she heard a wolf-whistle, she ignored it and alongside her ran a spotty faced lad, "at all reet" he asked. She looked at him and walked away, it was Reggie Lowe, cocky bugger. "What do you want" she shouted back at him, "Oh, now't" he answered skulking into the shadows. "Can't do with bloody idiots", she thought. "Just thought ye mite like to go out one nite", he bellowed. Cor what a bleedin cheek, "Sod off" she shouted at him "and dunna ask owt daft agin." Go out with 'im, never, "I'd rather be tied to a cows' tail and shit down," she snapped at him.

Once indoors she began the usual, helping with the kids and dishing up the food, hoping dad would be in a better mood. They all sat down to the meal nobody speaking a word, Jim always said "let your meat stop your mouth." So until you asked mam, "please may I leave the table you kept your mouth shut, til he'd gone anyway. Big Jim was very pensive tonight and was soon changed and out of the house. Probably off to see one of the women he's supposed to have, thought young Jim and Jean respectively. Still the atmosphere changed for the better when he went out. Young Jim and Harry were sat in the parlour later on talking about the government and what the Prime Minister was trying to do, Stanley Baldwin was a dirty word to a staunch Labour family and they argued to and fro.

There was cleaning to be done, so the girls all helped and it was done in no time. The little ones were put to bed and Camy sang a lullaby to Alex, he was such a little scamp and she loved him dearly as she loved all her brothers and sisters. She loved her mam too but never dared to show it, not Dad though, she couldn't remember him ever saying one kind word to her in all of her life. "He can bugger off", she said to herself, wishing with all her heart that he really would. Still suppose we're all to put up with whatever God brings us, now't we can do about it.

Mam was sewing by the fire when Camy came downstairs, she looked worn out and her eyes were straining at the trousers she was trying to patch up. "Shall I do em for ye mam?" she asked. Sal threw them over to her with not a word of thanks, she needed glasses really, but was too vain to have an eye test. "I'm just nippin' round to our Ada's'" she said, "look after the house", and she was gone. It was her only pleasure to sit and gossip with Ada and Ted so the girls didn't mind. Jean took the chance to go too, "I'll just go round to Annie's'" she shouted as she went through the door. They knew she meant Arthur Bennett's', still they didn't mind as long as mam and Dad didn't find out. Camy's' body shook from head to foot at the thought. Mary started to mend her stockings and Camy hummed quietly to herself, "The holly and the Ivy," she had it in her mind all day. Soon be Christmas, she smiled to herself, Don't know why I'm so happy about it now't good ever happens to me at Christmas or any other time. Dad would be pissed up as usual and be a bloody pig with them all, but the little ones would have a present, so it would be nice for them.

Young Jim shouted that he would be going out for an hour and Camy smiled again. Off to see his Tilly, he was a grand lad was their Jim, whatever would happen to him in the future wasn't clear. If their father was like other fathers he would have been married by now, not mooching about on the sly, frightened of Dad finding out. He would get a bloody good hidin' as old as he was. She sighed and picked up the patch for the trousers again, got to get them ready for Harry in the mornin', they were his only pair for work. She had a peg rug to do after the patching. The old coat had to be cut up and then cut into strips. The sacking was ready so it would be started before she went to bed.

Sal was surprised when young Jim came into the kitchen at Aunty Ada's. "Have you told her yet, aunty Ada?" he asked. "Told me what our Jim" snapped Sal, jumping up from the comfy chair by the fire. "Sit down lad and we can thrash it out." said aunty Ada. Sal looked puzzled, but waited for Ada to have her say first. She knew Ada and could see she had a story to tell and wouldn't be put off. "Right our Sal, things 'ave got to be said. Our Jim 'ere wants to get married." He asked me to have a word with you about it, "canna talk to that father of his, so its up to us, Sal", Sal wasn't really surprised by this news, she knew he was in love, she could read the signs, but if he got wed she would loose his money and she couldn't manage without it and Jim would go raving mad. "nar then, our Sal, I can see what yer thinkin' but it has to be faced." "I know that", said Sal, "but Jim, your Dad, how can you," she spluttered, young Jim hung his head and almost wept. "mam," he said "I dunna want ta leave thee wi Dad but I've got to find me own way in life, I'm twenty years old, they were married and had three kids at that age." "I know that," said Sal" but where will they live." At that Ada put her oar in "Tilly's' dad said they could live there for a time until they could find somewhere else." "When?" asked Sal looking into the eyes of her eldest son, he was a handsome your man, like his father in looks but without his temperament. Young Jim was a kind and gentle soul and she wished she could love him as a mother should but she darn't, she knew that. "Soon as we can mam, I'm gettin' a rise at work and I'll still bring some money round to you every week." Sal's shoulders hunched down, Ada and Ted went on and on, they had to get her approval to the idea. Give the young lad a bit of hope for the future. He was a good lad and deserved a helping hand, "Come on Sal, help him" implored Ada "please Sal, remember the time you needed help badly."

Ada hadn't meant to throw this up at Sal but she had to. Sal's eyes filled with tears remembering that time long ago when she had turned up on the doorstep. Her beloved William gone, her badly, her job, her home, her lifestyle, all gone, only a broken heart left to her. Ada and Ted recalled that picture too. She stood pale and stick thin looking like death warmed up, said Ada, not knowing what had happened to her and not knowing to this day. Sal told nobody, she hoped she would never have to. "Righto, she said after a long pause, "we must do it without lettin Jim know, He'll never agree, we all know that", "Oh no" said Ada "We're not scuttling about like bloody rats up ally. "I'll tell him, me and Ted, eh Ted." Ted agreed with Ada, "after all, if we go behind his back it'll be ten times worse for you lot left behind." It was agreed that Ted would speak to Jim and take him round to their house where Ada could work on him, he didn't dislike Ted and only ignored Ada because he knew she disapproved of him so strongly. The arrangements were made and Jim left to tell Tilly. Ada made them a strong cup of tea her remedy for everything. Ted would have preferred a good stiff whisky at the thought of his confrontation with big Jim Moore. They talked for some time and then Sal bade them goodnight and went off home.

By this time everyone was in bed except big Jim. She would have to wait up for him not knowing what state he would be in and having to lock the door and make sure the fire guard was in place. She picked up the rag rug that Camy had started, she had done about a quarter, good girl. They were all good kids, she didn't deserve them, she knew that. What sort of life had she given to any of them, and Jim, what had she done to him, he hated her, he had made her hate him, they never showed an ounce of love for any of their kids. She hated herself more than she hated anyone.

She fingered the cameo brooch in her breast pocket remembering "Oh, William, William," she thought her heart would break, never a day sent by that she didn't think about him, about his love, of their baby son. The thoughts of them both awaiting her in the afterlife kept her going," Until we meet again my darlings," she whispered. The door opened and a blast of cold night air filled the room, Jim reeled in bleary eyed, gave her a look of venom then headed for the stairs, kicking off his boots at the bottom, banging the door behind him. Sal gave him time to undress and get into bed, then she locked up, lit the candle, put out the gas light and made her way up the stairs with a heavy heart. She undressed and was just about to reach for her night-dress when she was aware that Jim was staring at her, his eyes feasting on her large round breasts, her slender hips and long legs in the candlelight. He reach for her and she shuddered as he took her roughly, no passion not a shred of tenderness, just pure unadulterated animal actions. First of all on her back and then he turned her over and had her from the rear, crushing her large breasts in his big hands until she almost screamed with pain. When he was spent he grunted, turned over and within seconds started to snore. She lay there used and bruised, hot tears streaming down. how many more years will I have to do this, she thought, why couldn't it be William, she thought about there lovemaking until she ached and twitched all over. She finally slept, dreaming she was still in the big house, she was running up the stairs on and on looking for William, going from room to room. There was Kitty with a baby in her arms. She ran to her but it was only a bundle of washing, Kitty laughed in her face, a hideous laugh, she ran on and on. Cook was there, she was pointing to the door, it must be William, she rushed to the door, it opened and she lunged down, down into blackness, as she plunged downwards she could hear their laughter ringing in her ears. She woke with a start, she was sweating and her heart was thumping so hard in her chest she thought it would wake Jim. She lay there trying to remember the dream. Kitty and Cook they had been just as they were when she had last seen them. Not aged like herself. I can't go on like this she thought, its not healthy, always to be reaching for the moon. The day will come soon enough when I shall be with my loved ones.

CHAPTER

6

Sleep didn't come easy to young Jim, he was wide awake, thoughts of the day going around in his head. He'd been wise to engage the help of Aunty Ada, a very wise move. She understood them all so well, why couldn't mam be like Aunty Ada. What was wrong with her, he never had a hug or a kiss from her in all his twenty years. Lots from Aunty Ada, none from mam, he sometimes wished Aunty Ada was his mam but felt guilty and tried not to think about it. He had rushed round to his Tilly soon after tea. She was as thrilled as he was they had kissed passionately and hungrily, he groaned deeply, how much longer could they keep from going the whole way with each other. They did everything but. They were determined to wait until they were wed and getting on their feet before bearing any children.

Tilly was a good girl and taught at the Sunday School every weekend, she loved the little ones and they all loved her. She was kind and thoughtful, a good help to her mam and Dad. They had both been a bit upset when Tilly and Jim has asked them about getting wed, but getting to know Jim better agreed he really was a grand lad. The reputation of his father wasn't what they would have wanted, but all things considered they both said yes that they would help the young pair as much as they possibly could. They would live at the Bennett's and have Tilly's' bedroom, a double bed would have to be bought, plus linen. There was lots to be done, the church to be booked, reception arranged, the dress to be made, flowers, cake. "Oh Lord", said Mrs. Bennett, "so much to do, would Mrs. Moore be getting involved", she asked, Jim was a little downcast, "I don't really know yet Mrs. Bennett, I can't rightly say just now. I'll speak to her about it but Dad will....", he didn't finish, couldn't explain about what Dad was like. "Aunty Ada will help" said Jim "his face lit up, she always helped everyone, yes Aunty Ada would help, even if mam and Dad wouldn't. He would speak to Aunty Ada about it tomorrow.

He tossed and turned in his bed, things would turn out alreet he knew that soon, he hoped, very soon, then he would have his Tilly beside him in bed every night to make love to, to kiss, to hold. He'd never made love it frightened him, but he surely wanted to try it out more and more each day, he never thought about much else these days. He had a permanent hard on, he only hoped no one would notice. The thought of Tilly's young swollen breasts, nipples hard and enticing were too much for Jim to bear, he began to masturbate as quickly as he possible could, trying not to wake Harry who shared his bed. He shuddered strongly and came quickly, his heart pounding at least now he would sleep, he wanted to dream of Tilly and their wedding. Sleep came to him at last and he snored softly, tomorrow was another day after all.

Morning came quickly enough, everyone was up and about talking about Christmas, Joe, Lizzie and Alex were so excited, wondering what Santa would be bringing them. Big Jim was in a foul mood, "Shut you're bloody traps or yer'll get fuck all", he bellowed. The girls lowered their heads, they hated him more than ever when he talked like that, it was OK to say words like that telling a tale or having a joke, but not to be shouting at your kids. He really was distasteful.

When they had all left for there days toil or school Ada was round to talk about the forthcoming wedding plans. "I can't help, you know that Ada. Jim will never let me help them and he keeps the money. I only have what he allows, what canna do to help, I can't feed me kids proper, never mind pay for fancy weddings." "I'll have to do everything then, shall I Sal, always bloody well left up to me, I'd better speak wi' Ted about it." She lit up a fag and puffed deeply, what a friggin' carry on, Ted would be mad it was always left up to them two to take all the shit. Ada was livid, "They're non my bloody kids", she barked. "I haven't bloody well got any friggin kids, I should have a dozen and let someone else pay for 'em and look after 'em, ey I've slipped up badly done everything arse way round." Sal watched her seethin'. She was right, it wasn't her war to fight, but Sal couldn't fight Jim, not now, not ever. Besides she wasn't well enough for some time now, she had been having little black outs, nothing much, but a bit worrying. She hadn't told anyone, didn't want to worry any of them, most of all Ada. "What would I do without you Ada," she murmured, her eyes misting over. "Don't start piping your bloody eyes, our Sal", said Ada. "W'll do what has to be done, I will bake and you can sew, make 'em some embroidered pillowcases, that 'ed be nice", said Ada. "Reet", said Sal, "Yes, I can do that alreet." Ada said she would ask Ted to go round to the Bennett's that night and find out what was being arranged. She would let Sal know, then Ted would speak to Jim. They had a cup of tea and Ada told Sal about Fred Wright, Jean had told Uncle Ted, if he touches that lass or the others Ted had said, "I'll bloody well castrate the bloody tom cat." Sal sighed, her girls were grown up, they would have to go through all that, she had gone through. "Lets hope they don't find a Jim Moore", said Sal. "Amen to that," echoed Ada, "Amen to that."

So it was that Ada and Ted went round that night to the Bennett's' house, Ted wouldn't go alone. Tom and Ethel greeted them warmly, "sit thee sen's down, will yer have a cup of tea", asked Ethel. When they had settled with a cuppa in the neat clean parlour, Tom asked why Jim's Mam hadn't come round, was she poorly. "No" answered Ada "but you must bear with us, our Sal's' husband, Jim is a funny man, and its hard to talk to him about anything, You must know about Jim Moore they both said, but dunna take it owt on our young Jim, a finer lad yer're never met." It was agreed that Ada and Ted would keep in touch with Tom and Ethel and pass on any arrangements to Sal about the Wedding. Ada would do the lions share of the baking and loaning of pots, cups and saucers and cutlery etc. They agreed thirty guests would receive invitations and the Bennett's parlour would be used for the wedding breakfast. They would get Christmas over with and then concentrate on saving flour, eggs, sugar etc. Ada would bake the cake, she was noted for her mouth-watering refreshments and her fruit cake was envied throughout the town. Icing sugar and colouring would have to be scrounged from hither and thither. February 28th would be the date, so they had plenty of time to get everything in motion. Ted would be calling to see Jim the next night. He would ask him round to their house and break the news to him there.

Wednesday morning dawned cold and crisp, a smattering of snow had fallen in the night. Little Alex had climbed into Camy's' bed again and pee'd up her back, she shot out of bed, not again, for Christ's sake, I'm bleedin fed up wi this. Down the stairs as quiet as a mouse, the candle lit and the clock struck five-thirty, it wasn't too bad. She was dying for a pee, so she cocked her bum over the kitchen sink and had one there, it was too cold for the outside lavy. She ran cold water to wash it away and laughed to herself, Dad and mam would bloody kill her if they knew she had pee'd in't the sink, but it only made her giggle more than ever. She felt like she'd got one over on them both. She washed and dressed and got the porridge ready, putting out the dishes and spoons. By the time the porridge was ready everyone was getting up. "What's up, pee'd yer bed", said mam as she came into the kitchen. "Alex did it for me", she answered, "you shouldn't let im inter yer bed, its yer own doin." she told

Camy. "Yer'll get fed up with it soon enough, when yer smell like a bloody lavy."

The morning went along quietly enough Jim was thoughtful and moody and just grunted, ate his porridge, grabbed his snap bag, coat, scarf and hat and was gone, followed by young Jim and Harry. Jean, Mary and Camy left for the shed clattering down the cobbled street. Camy in her too big brown shoes, which were soon swapped over for her comfy plimsolls. mam would never know that her bargain shoes, only went to and fro from the shed.

The same routine warp, weft, weavers knot, but she sang the popular songs of the day at the top of her voice, no one could hear her above the noise of the looms, so it helped to pass the time more quickly. Jessie seemed to be please with her today, "Yer trying lass, that the main thing, keep on tryin it'll come to thee soon enough, yer'll wonder why you couldn't do it right away, its so easy, when you know how." She went off down the shed smiling to herself, must be off to have a bit with shitty Fred, silly cow, thought Camy. What does she do, when he breaths on her, bloody hell, its enough to make her faint or be sick. Someone called her loudly and beckoned her over to a group of women, "come and have a look" she said. Camy went over an old girl was holding a drawing of a naked man, "look at the size of his dick", she laughed, it was enormous, hanging right down to his knees and his balls massive. They all fell about laughing, Camy blushed beetroot red, she had never seen anything like that before, " Jesus Christ " she said "do they grow that big" the old girl laughed even harder. "I wish they did lass, I wish they did," her one and only tooth stuck out from her gums and seemed to shake about. Camy couldn't keep her eyes off it. "It's me pittler stabber", she laughed "me pittler stabber" and rocked from side to side. Camy rushed back to her looms. There was the biggest mess she had ever seen, the whole front of the cloth was in a terrible state. She stopped it and looked around wondering what the hell to do. One of the old girls saw her face. "What's up lass", she asked rushing over, looked at the loom, called another woman. She sent Camy over to watch her looms and set about un-weaving the mess, they worked like hell and had almost finished when Jessie came back, luckily, she was in a good mood, so she finished off. "Can't bloody well leave yer for two minutes", she snarled at Camy, "Do's yer mam like yer looking at naked men, eh." Camy was terrified she would tell mam, Jessie looked at her frightened face, she wouldn't say anything, but she had a lesson to learn. "You thing less about men's dicks and more about gettin yer work done proper" she chided and left it at that. Mrs one tooth smiled across at her and the others who had started on the Monday with her stared and smirked at her. "Your bleedin time will come", she mouthed at them "just you wait."

That night, right after tea Uncle Ted came round, it was a bit unusual for him to call when big Jim was in the house, "how do, Ted" said big Jim, "how do" said Ted back, "I've got sommat to say ter yer Jim, can yer come round ter our house." Jim was a bit taken aback, "what for, Ted?" Ted stammered and stuttered, "Won't take long Jim if you'll be coming round", Jim had respect for Ted always had, so he reached for his cap and jacket, he looked round at all of them, thinking, which one of em was in bloody trouble. Round to Ada's they went, big Jim walking tall behind small fat Ted, Ada watched as they came in through the door. "Sit down Jim" said Ada, "No thanks I'll stand, if yer dunna mind. Who's done summat wrong then?" he asked, looking at Ted. "Nobody has done wrong Jim, I want you to hear Ada out. Listen to what she has to say, then you can add your penneth." So Jim looked straight at Ada, she was feeling uncomfortable under his stare, she cleared her throat. "I can't talk with you two standing over me, sit down" she barked, more if fear than anything else. They sat, she went on to tell Jim about his son and Tilly Bennett. "He's twenty years old, Jim and he wants to get wed, now its no use you rantin" and ravin', he's a grown man, Jim, so do the right thing for once in your life and give the lad a chance, help him."

Jim sat there seething as Ada told him of the plans they had made. When she had finished, she sat with arms folded, "right its your turn Jim, what do'st say?" asked Ted, well pleased. Jim standing up, " looks to me like you've got it all cut and dried, now't for me to bloody well do is there if the sneaky little bastard wants to get himself wed then let 'im is the lass in't family way, he sneered, "anyway he can get out of my bloody house tonight, I won't have sneaky buggers under my bleedin' roof." "Now Jim," said Ted brusquely "No need for that language in front of Ada. Oh no, mustn't upset Ada, must we. "What about Sal what does she say?" " Oh, she's too feared oh thee to say owt", answered Ada. "Everything left to other folk, anyone but you lot," she was stung by his attitude, there was no need to react like this after all they had one. He should be thankful, but no, a shit to the bitter end was Jim Moore.

He stood at the door, Ted asked him once more "Jim, think about what yer sayin', he didn't ask to be born yer know. Its not his fault yer don't like im. Let im have a little bit of happiness he, life's a bugger at best of times." Jim didn't know how to answer this. He stood with his head downcast and after some thought he said, "Righto, Ada, do what yer want, I'll say nowt but don't expect me to attend this nice little family get together." Her face was a picture, she looked like a bloody battleship in full sail, thought Jim and would have laughed if it wasn't so serious. With that he was gone. Ada started to cry, "the bastard", she cried, "the bloody cruel rotten swine, why did our Sal marry such a bloody rotter? Ted you'd better fetch our young Jim and get his things here, he'll have to get married from here, that bugger will kill him tonight when he gets in, tanked up. Ted ran round and told the story to Sal and young Jim. Camy took the younger ones upstairs out of the way, while Jim gathered up his belongings. He didn't want to leave mam, but they told him he must go. "Come for me mam, if he starts," said Jim "promise me." Promise she did. "I'll be alreet, go with Uncle Ted", she urged him. The door closed on them leaving a sharp cold wind behind, Sal was afraid, Jim would go berserk when he came home, she clutched at the cameo brooch, what would become of her eldest son, he would never ever sleep in the house again, he was gone forever, her son, Jim. He had done the right thing, it's time he was wed, yes, he had done the right thing. He would be safe with Ada and Ted, but would the rest of them? Sal urged the others to get to bed before he came home, they had been talking amongst themselves and wondering what to do for the best. They were all afraid and went to bed too scared to sleep, to scared not to. It was after midnight before big Jim returned. They heard him falling up the stairs. Luckily he was too drunk to do anything, so they all sighed with relief.

The next morning they sat together for the first time without their beloved brother, Jim. Tears were in their eyes, a lump in their throats. Dad looked at them one by one, "right you bleedin lot, your brother has decided to leave us, so I dona want ye to speak 'is name in this house ag'in. Do you all hear!" They all jumped as he hit the table with his fists. Cups overturned, spoons clattered. "Do yer hear me?" "Yes dad." They all shouted back, even the little ones. "Right that's it then and don't you bloody well forget it." The door closed behind him and Harry reached down his hat and scarf, he hadn't slept much last night, he missed Jim. He'd miss the warmth of him and the bed was empty without the big brother he had slept with all of his life. "Tar-ra mam", he said " shall I say owt to our Jim for yer." "No nothin' lad, there's now't to be said, you heard what yer father said. Go on or yer'll; be late fer work." Harry left, his heart heavy, what would Dad and Jim do when they met at work. He hoped they didn't fight. He didn't want Jim to be hurt. If that bastard hits our Jim I'll go for 'im, thought Harry. He hated his Dad even more today than ever, what would the day bring.

CHAPTER

7

It was show-down time at Bridgevale Foundry. Young Jim arrived first of all, he hadn't slept a wink all night. He was in his mothers old room, Aunty Ada had given him the history if it, nothing had been moved since the days of young Sally Smith. He counted the stippled pattern on the walls over and over gain until he thought he would go mad. He was glad to get up as soon as he dare stir. Didn't want to wake up Aunty Ada and Uncle Ted, who looked at him with heavy hearts.

What would happen at the foundry, he couldn't eat any breakfast, he felt sick to his stomach, he wanted to cry, but daren't. He missed Harry and mam and the rest of the kids. Now he would have to face Dad, he was bloody terrified, he took up his snap bag, coat , scarf and cap. Ada hugged him to her, "if that bugger touches you, I'll be up there and kick is arse", she said through a mist of tears. "It'll be alreet Aunty Ada, don't worry yer sen. See mam is alreet will yer. I worried all night wondering if he'd hit her." "Aye lad, so did we," said uncle Ted, "If he did it'll be the last time. I shall have him put out once and for all."

Young Jim's feet were heavy as lead climbing up the hill, it was still dark, gas lamps cast their eerie glow and hissed out an un-named tune. It was slippery and once or twice he nearly lost his footing. Two more days to Christmas, what kind of Christmas would they have, he wished he hadn't met Tilly then none of this would be happening. No, he didn't, Tilly was his life, he couldn't live without her, footsteps sounded behind him running fast, he turned sharply, expecting to see his Dad, it was one of the new hands afraid of being late. "How do, Jim, at all reet." "Oh, aye," answered Jim, trying not to show his fear, "I'm right champion," he blathered "How yer doin' on then?" he asked the young lad. "Dunna like it much, too bloody dirty and smelly, I'll get used to it me Dad says. I'll get me arse kicked if I get the sack." Jim didn't answer his mind was elsewhere, the lad looked up at him and wondered if he was all there. Jim hung up his bag, coat, cap and scarf and donned his overalls and went through to his place of work. Big Jim arrived a couple of minutes later. His son looked up at him, "Oh, Christ almighty", thought young Jim this is it. His guts began to churn and he felt sick. His knees wobbled and he held on to a chain dangling from the ceiling for support. He remembered the phase 'shitting yerself' well, now he knew exactly what it meant. Big Jim towered over him, his face contorted with rage. "Right lad, yer don't live under my roof any longer, you've packed yer bags and slunk off like a bloody big lass, so piss off to yer new family, don't ever come round the house again. I don't want to see yer bleedin face anywhere near us, you've turned yer back on us all. Your mam and the rest of us. You've taken the food from them little ones mouths and I hope you're proud of yerself." "But Dad you said I was to go. I don't want to do it like this , canna we sort it out like. I can give mam some money every week it's just that," he didn't finish off. Big Jim smacked him in the mouth and he fell to the ground like a leaf in autumn. "Don't you bloody well insult me lad," he snarled "from now on yer on yer own." With that his father turned and marched off. A couple of the men had been watching, ready to defend the lad if need be, one of them helped him up and he started to cry, he felt humiliated, "that bastard" he spluttered "I'm bloody well finished wi im", young Harry came rushing in "Jim" he shouted. At last the two bothers held each other tight like brothers should, not ashamed to say that they loved one another. The foreman came through, having heard of the rumpuss. Go and get a brew you two, and dunno rush back. They were fine young lads and didn't deserve a bloody bastard like Jim Moore for a father, but he was the best worker they had, so they had to grin and bear it. They would have to make sure that the three didn't work together. It was a big place so it shouldn't be too difficult thought Mr. Lashley, the Forman.

That evening Jim Moore sat down at his table and before any dared to eat a bite, he told them in no uncertain terms that young Jim would not be welcome in the house and that they were to have nothing more to do with him or, but God he would want to know the reason why. Anyone who did could pack their bags and follow him down the road. No one answered back, they ate in silence. Even Alex and Lizzie and Ted understood that when Dad was mad they shut their mouths and stayed quiet and still until he had gone out. Harry wanted to smash his Dad's face in but knew he was no match for the big strong man, but one day he swore, my time will come. Sal could feel herself falling and hung onto the chair. She felt week and giddy. Better get some food inside me, she thought. I haven't eaten today. I wonder how things were at the foundry, couldn't get a bite down her. Ada was round soon as Jim went out of the door. "Well it's a fine bloody kettle of fish to be sure, our Sal." she said. "I can't see him letting any of you to th' wedding, can you?" Sal nodded her head, "don't think he will Ada. What shall we do, poison the bugger for't the big day." They could have laughed if there had been out to laugh at.

The girls were all upset, we can't let our Jim get wed and not go, we have to go, he's our Jim, I miss him," said Lizzie and began to howl, which made Alex wail too. Jean, Mary and Camy wiped the tears from their eyes and got on with the washing up. "Two bloody days to Christmas", said Ada "what a shitty Christmas it will be, I'm sure." Still the cake had to be iced so Ada set about that, and Sal was busy getting out the Christmas tree and decorations, while Camy had to put the little ones to bed. They were all upset and clung to Camy, "You won't go away and leave us will you Cam?" they asked their big eyes shimmering in the candlelight. "No babies, I won't leave you, no one will want to marry me anyway, so dunna ya worry." After three bedtime stories they were asleep and she tiptoed down the stairs. mam had decorated the small tree and it looked lovely, they would make some paper chains tomorrow night. Ada finished the icing and they all sang her praises, it looked really good and they couldn't wait to cut into it.

Camy was so tired so she went up to bed, it had been a long day and there would be another one tomorrow and the next. Then the Christmas holidays, that would be Saturday, Christmas day which was a Sunday, Boxing day on the Monday was also a bank holiday. So three days before work re-started, it would be bliss, sheer bliss, thought Camy as she drifted into a deep well earned sleep.

Thursday morning dawned crisp and cold, cold outside and even colder inside. Cold silence from Jim to his family. He hadn't spoke to them since tea time last night. No one had dared to speak first. , After a silent breakfast he went off to work followed shortly by Harry who would never walk by his side again. In his heart his Dad was dead, just a thing existed, a madman, a wife beater, a child batterer, everything but a father. He's no Dad of mine anymore he chanted to himself over and over again as he climbed up the hill to work. One day I will be the man and he had better watch out.

Ada came round that morning to see what had been going on in the house with Jim. "He hasn't spoken a word", said Sal, "just stared into space and sulked like a big soft kid". "What's to be told to the Bennett's, that's what I want to know " asked Ada, "Dunna ask me, I don't bloody well know" shouted back Sal, "we can't go the weddin, none of us or else he'll bloody well kill us all." It was decided after half a dozen cups of tea and four fags that Ada and Ted would go to the Bennett's later on in the day and see what was to be done about the weddin'. It would be better if they set a new date for later on in the year to give Jim time to come to terms with it, perhaps accept it. They knew they were clutching at straws but anything would be worth trying.

After tea Ada and Ted duly went round to see the Bennett's, meeting young Jim on the way, they trouped into the parlour and sat down to discuss what was the best thing to do under the circumstances. Tom and Ethel were very concerned about Sal and the kids, " we can't let anything happen to them they said." conjuring up thoughts of dire beatings in their midst. After a long discussion the wedding date was re-arranged for the 28th August. That would give Jim Moore plenty of time to cool down and behave himself. Ada and Ted couldn't thank them enough, "what nice people they are" said Ada as they walked home. Our Jim will be well loved by all of them. She fastened her scarf tightly round her neck to keep out the bitter cold and linked Ted's arm a bit tighter. He looked round at her and saw the tears glistening in her eyes, eh by heck lass yer'l piss less he teased her." "Oh Ted, I'm that lucky to ave you, and a few more tears fell in appreciation."

They arrived back home to find Jean at their door, "Oh, aunty Ada" she shouted. "mam's poorly, she passed out at the table." Ada and Ted rushed into Sal's. They had put her on the settle in't parlour, even big Jim was hovering about. Ada sailed right past him, didn't care if he was in a bad mood or good. "Sal", she cried "Sal, whatevers up wi yer," Sal was as white as chalk and couldn't speak to her. "Its alreet Sal, doctors on his way," said Jim. Ada looked up at him and couldn't believe her eyes. She had never seen that tender look in his eyes in all the twenty years they had been married. If I didn't know better, I'd swear he cared for her deeply, thought Ada.

The doctor arrived and gave Sal the once over, asked her questions, she finally managed to tell him she had been feeling dizzy for some weeks now and she hadn't been eating very much, it made her feel sickly. He listened to her heart, felt her pulse, looked into her eyes with a light, felt all over her stomach, then he cleared his throat and looked up at them all. "I think Mrs. Moore has had a slight heart attack," he stated. "She must not be moved for several days, and nursed day and night for about a week. Can you arrange for someone to look after the little ones?" he asked. They had a job to take it all in, panic seized them. " she's dying ", they thought, "No not mam," "No not my sister." The doctor cleared his throat again. "She is in no danger at the moment and with rest and care she will make a full recovery" he said. That was what they wanted to hear. "Oh yes doctor" they chorused. All flying into action, making tea and plumping up cushions. Ada was beside herself, she couldn't lose her Sal, she loved her too much. "Right Jean, you'll have to stay off work for a week or two. I'll come round every mornin' and help wi' kids, they finish school tomorra for the Christmas holidays. I'll do the washing etc, and the cooking, you girls will have to help your mam when I go home at night, is that understood." They all agreed. Jim said he would sit with Sal the night. He wasn't tired he said and he could go in late in the morning. Everyone was surprised, but said now't.

The doctor left giving instructions about some pills he had left her. "Keep her as quiet as you can and she'll be as right as rain." he declared. "Goodnight all" he doffed his hat and was gone. Harry wanted to know everything he had been with the kids and couldn't hear what was being said. Ada explained the procedure to him and said, Jim was staying with her in the parlour tonight, so everyone would be quiet, kids put to bed and the chores done with the least possible noise.

The girls looked at each other, they had never felt so scared, they bustled round doing all the jobs that had to be done and seeing Ada off home with Ted, who tutted and shook his head. "That lass has come to the end of her tether Ada, you mark my words, she canna go on like this not anymore she canna." "We'll do all we can Ted" sniffed Ada, "I can't loose her she's all I have besides you," she began to weep and Ted put his arms around her. "Come on, lass, dunna fret now, no use you makin' yer sen bad, you've got to keep yer strength up to help your Sal. Hush now, its a warning, she'll be alreet if she's looked after so lets get to bed we've a long day ahead. Pots to do and Christmas presents to wrap, Turkey to get from the farm and the mince pies won't bake themselves eh, old girl." "Eh Ted, your a tonic, don't know what I would do without yer," mumbled Ada. Ted put out the milk for their cocoa.

Jim Moore looked down on his stricken wife, he was terrified she was going to die. He couldn't bear to loose her even if he hated her for what she had done to him, in his heart he knew it was love he felt not hate, but he would never admit it, not ever. He sat in his chair by the fire and Sal slept for the first night on the settle. It was quite comfy and she slept well. The doctor pill had done her good. Why was Jim sat there with her it wasn't natural for him to show any feelings. Perhaps he was doing it for show, pretending to care in front of the doctor. Didn't want to loose face did he.

Jim didn't sleep at all that night, he went over and over the last twenty years with Sally, wondering how long he would have her with him, it was a frightening time. He was as scared as the rest of them. He would do his best if he could, one a rotter always a rotter he said to himself. He knew what he was no one had to spell it out for Jim Moore.

The next morning everyone was up early, relieved that their mam was still alive. Ada came round at seven o'clock and everything went like clockwork. She went into the parlour with a cup of tea for Sal and propped her up with plenty of pillows. "How art feeling, our Sal" she cooed. Sal answered weakly "I'm fine Ada, don't you go worrying about me, I'm tough as old boots," they smiled at each other warmly. Knowing this was not really the truth, Ada swallowed a lump in her throat. "Santa comes round tonight Sal, ave yer hung yer stocking up?" Not waiting for an answer she went one, "me and Jean will wrap the littlens presents up and put them in't glory ole." Sal nodded, she didn't have the strength to care, one way or t'other. Ada washed her hands and face. She'd bought round her best flannel and a nice soft fluffy towel. "Shall we change yer nightie our Sal?" she asked "Not yet" answered Sal, " in a bit Ada, righto" said Ada kissing Sal's pale cold cheek, "right" she said and closed the parlour door.

"Yer mam's having forty winks, so lets get doin'" gabbled Ada, trying not to cry again. The little ones went off to school thinking of Santa tonight. Not really understanding about mam being poorly. Jim went to work late and young Jim dashed back from work to see mam for a little while, frightened his Dad would walk in and see him there.

"It's my fault, Aunty Ada, if I hadn't started this would never have happened" he said, his large brown eyes looking like saucers. "Now dunna do blamin' yer sen," scolded Ada "I'll have none of it, do yer hear me, don't say it agin. It'll upset yer mam if she ears yer, now think on lad."

There was a knock at the door, it was Doctor Hallam, Ada let him in. "How's the patient" he enquired. "Resting nicely, doctor", said Ada, come through. He had a look at Sal, listened to her heart again, checked her pulse. "Now, Mrs Moore", he said you can go upstairs to your bedroom and I want you to stay in bed for at least a week. Will you promise me you will do that?" Sal nodded her head. "If you do as your told, you will get well very quickly, if not it could be very serious for you. Rest and quite, I know it's not going to be easy but you really must try. You have got a lot of helpers so it will take the weight off your shoulders. Right then I'm leaving these pills and take them like the others I left you last night, I will see you in a day or two. Good morning." he beckoned Ada into the kitchen. "I'd like Mr. Moore to call into the surgery to see me, so would you tell him? Thank you, good day to you" and he was gone. Wonder what he wants Jim for and she felt panic rising in her breast. "Ada" shouted Sal "come and help me upstairs. With Ada and Jean they managed to get up the stairs. She was a dead weight, so weak she couldn't stand unaided. They lowered her into bed and fussed around her till she was comfy. Then they left her to have a sleep. "Ey plenty of rest will do the trick," said Ada hopefully. I'll make some tea and a fruit cake." Ada said to Jean, that would keep her busy for a few hours. She left Jean to wrap the Christmas gifts and set off to the butchers for some discount beef and a few other odds and ends for Christmas dinner. Ted would get the turkey. They would have to have it all together this year, with Sal being poorly. What would Jim have to say about that she wondered. He could say what he bloody well wanted, it didn't matter it would have to be done that way, Oh hell, what about young Jim. He was banned from the house, they couldn't leave him out, Oh God Almighty what were they goin' to do. That Jim Moore had a lot to answer for, he had.

She would have a word with Ted and young Jim when she got chance later on tonight. One thing was for sure, Sal would not have any worry, she was far too poorly, she might have died. Ada caught her breath, Oh Sal, my Sal, what would I do without you. She loved her sister very much and often wondered about her life in London. She had come back that day white and drawn and never said a word about what went wrong. But Ada had seen the sparkle had gone out of her eyes, they looked dead, she had always hoped that Sal would tell her one day, when she was ready, but after twenty years she had given up hope and didn't really thing about it any more. She had married Jim Moore in a hurry with young Jim on the way, but why had she rushed into a relationship so soon after returning home. It was beyond Ada. Now Sal was poorly and would need constant care and attention, and Ada would see that she got it. It would be hard work, but she was no stranger to that and her Ted would help her, she could count on Ted he was the best.

CHAPTER

8

Jim Moore had a message to call on Doctor Hallam, so he called into the surgery on the way home from work. He didn't have to wait , the last patient had just gone. "Come in Jim" said Doctor Hallam, he was a small friendly man in his sixties. Bald and bespectacled, very neat and tidy with shoes polished till you could see your face in them. "Right Jim, I'll get straight to the point, your wife has suffered quite a bad heart attack, not bad enough to hospitalise her, but she will need lots of care and attention. However, there is one thing I really must stress to you. She must have no more babies if she did, it would kill her, she isn't strong enough to go through it. Now I know its not easy but there are aids to prevent this happening, so if you want help I can help you along those lines." Jim sat very quiet, "That's OK doctor, there won't be any need for aids, you don't need to worry. I won't put Sal's life at risk, ye can be sure o that. The doctor could tell by his eyes that the man meant every word he said. There would be no need to worry. "Right that's fine then, I'll see you out Jim, remember she must stay in be for a week or two at least and take all her medication, I'll be around in a day or so." "Good night doctor and thank you."

Jim was deep in thought, from this day on he would never again have sex with Sal, he would not be responsible for her loosing her life, never that, so no more babies, no more nights wanting her and taking her, hurting her because of his hurt. His heart was heavy at the though but he could get everything he wanted elsewhere and he would do so, he couldn't imagine life without Sal, no matter what had happened over the years. No matter how they had hated each other, no matter how he had hit her, thrashed her in drink, belittled her in front of the kids, kept her short of money, he knew how he had wronged her, but whatever he had done he couldn't ever imagine life without her.

Sal laid back in her bed, Ada had put on her best covers and sheets and pillowcases it felt warm and snug and she was enjoying the rest. She had only rested between babies and it was really strange lying here without a baby at her side and the worry of another mouth to feed. She recalled the day before when she had felt so poorly, of how she had such pains in her chest and had passed out. Right down on the floor, remembering how they had rushed to her, how Jim had picked her up like she was made of china and put her on the settle in the parlour, had given instructions left right and centre. She had seen the panic in his eyes and couldn't believe what she saw. He cares about me after all these years, he still cares. She thought that she was going to die, but William wasn't waiting for her, she always thought he would be, so it was a bit of a shock to find he wasn't there. Anyway she had rallied round so perhaps she wasn't ready yet. Yes, that was it, he wasn't waiting because it wasn't her time yet. Poor Ada, she would have everything to do with it being Christmas, but the girls would be a good help and even the little ones would do their bit. Young Jim had been to see her, he was so scared she was going to die, it was written all over him. "Jim, I'll be alreet. Dunna you fret,"she said for the tenth time. "What will you do for Christmas day, Ada and Ted are cooking round here are you goin' to come here." "No mam, I'm goin' to the Bennett's, Tilly asked me last night, do yer mind mam. Will it be alreet?" "Eh, Jim it'll be champion dunna you worry." Jim could see she was tired and got up to leave, "right I'm off now mam, I'll see you sometime tomorrow, when he goes out, tar ra mam." He wanted to kiss her cheek but couldn't. he had never done it so didn't know how to. He went down stairs to Ada and told her of his plans for Christmas day, "Aye lad its best, don't want any trouble when big 'ead goes out," she laughed, he laughed at that "Ye he is a bloody big 'ead, tar ra Aunty Ada, see yer at bedtime.

Ada got on with the tea, there was lots to do. Jean was aright good help, so they had everything tik a boo by the time everyone sat down at the table. "You don't have any objections to Ted and me making Christmas dinner round here Jim?" she asked him he looked up from his tasty grub. "What a good cook Ada was, he couldn't fault that. "Well its for the best I dare say Ada, with Sal unable." He didn't like help from anybody, but this time it couldn't be helped. So they agreed reluctantly nice to each other. He was responsible for Sal being poorly, she knew that and she hated him for it, but the kids had enough misery and torment so she would bide her time, before she told him exactly what she thought of him.

These kids would have a good Christmas this year even if their mam was poorly. Ada was up late seeing to the bits and bobs that needed doing, the little ones had hung up their stockings round the parlour fireplace. The tree looked nice and a few paper chains were strung round the room. Ada wondered if Jim would rip them down when he came in. He had gone out after his meal without a word. She wondered what the doctor had wanted him for, he hadn't mentioned it and she wouldn't ask him.

Fancy going out when your wife was ill, still what else could she expect from someone like him. Jean, Mary and Camy had filled the stockings and they went off to bed. There would be an early start tomorrow, no lie in for Camy like she had hoped for, maybe Sunday. They had each called in to see their mam and say goodnight. She looked pale and thin and they were filled with heartache. "Please get better" they all prayed, "don't leave us." The though of mam dying was too much to bear, they went to bed dreading the day when mam would no longer be there with them. Big Jim came home later than ever that night, he had been in bed with Meg, he told her he would be seeing a lot more of her in the future. He had to get it somewhere, he was used to regular sex and couldn't do without it and if he couldn't ever have Sal again, he would have Meg or Ginny who he knew wanted him really bad. , So he wouldn't be going short in that department. None the less it wouldn't be the same. Sal's body was to him like heaven, but never again, unless she got better and had that operation so she wouldn't have any more kids. Still that wouldn't come for some years. So better not dwell on it. No never again was what he had to think about now. Sal was sleeping peacefully and for the first time in their twenty years he slipped into bed quietly, so as not to disturb her. Before he'd banged around burping and farting, not giving a tuppeny dam but tonight was different. Sal needed her rest if she was to get better.

Christmas morning dawned and everyone was up early. Jim was sat in the parlour at seven o'clock with a brew of tea, Joe, Teddy Lizzie and Alex rushed down the stairs to pick up their stockings. They were shushed from every quarter to be quiet, "Mams poorly", they crept into the parlour to see Dad sitting there. They came back out quickly, so Jean went and got the stockings for them, "are you alreet, Dad" she said not really expecting a reply. "Oh, I'm alreet Jean", he answered "thanks," she looked at him, by gum, he must be feeling poorly too. He didn't look too good it wasn't like him to be so quiet, he wasn't cursing and ranting. Perhaps he cared about mam after all. He'd left it a bit bloody late though. The kids were waiting for their Christmas stockings, so she left him to it. They were excited and happy with their small gifts, their little toys and orange, apple and nuts, a few sweets and some hankies for mam. They took them upstairs and wished mam a happy Christmas, she looked a bit better this morning and wanted to get up, but was told to behave and stay where she was or else Aunty Ada would be sent for. No need to send for her, she sailed in with Ted carrying the turkey and her with everything to make the Christmas dinner. One to remember, she went to see Sal and gave her a big kiss and hug. "Merry Christmas our Sal, I will be up with your dinner when its ready, till then you can read something or just rest up." Sal told her she was feeling a lot better, Ada was pleased but forbade her to set foot out of bed except for a wee.

Jim went for a walk round while they bustled about with the dinner, he couldn't take anymore of the clap trap going on. One or two of the neighbours asked after Sal, "She's middlin', thanks." he said. Jim was not prepared to stop and chat, that was for women not him. He walked down to the canal to the very spot where he had taken Sal on their first date together. What a night, talk about the agony and the ecstasy one had followed another. Their lovemaking had never been like that first night it had been like nothing he had ever known before or since the height of passion he had felt for Sal only to know that she thought he was someone else, her William, well Sal you almost destroyed me that night and have got yourself a bitter and twisted man, a man who because of what happened has beaten you, made you so sour that you couldn't even love your own children as neither could I. He began to weep quietly to himself, something he hadn't done for twenty years, since that terrible time which had started here on this canal bank, all that time ago. He wept for himself most of all and for Sal and their offspring's, none born of love, all born of carnal lust and sheer bloody mindedness. He stayed there awhile watching the swans, noticing how the ice was getting thicker over the surface of the canal, the bloody daft kids would be playing on it like they always did and it wasn't safe, but it was now't to do with him so let them get on with it, he had enough bleedin problems as it was without trying to save mankind. He dried his eyes and set off back home.

The dinner would be ready soon, he'd have to get to the pub and have a few drinks before he faced the family gathering. Jesus Christ what a bloody Christmas, he wondered if life was worth living, still if he had a few pints he would be able to face anyone never mind the bloody battleship, Ada. It was a nice walk down to the canal, he hadn't walked much before only to work and the pub. Sal would have liked it he thought, don't talk bloody rubbish man, he said to himself, she wouldn't like it at all, she wouldn't like to do anything with him. Perhaps with that bastard

William she would have strolled along on a Sunday afternoon, Oh yes, perhaps she would have been a different woman with the man she loved, he entered the pub, he was where he was happiest. The good company, Meg was there she was all woman just what he needed at the moment, he wondered how he was going to keep his hands off her until tonight, yes, life wasn't all bad, was it.

Everyone was ready at the dinner table, Ted was waiting to carve the turkey, but Jim hadn't arrived. Ada was stamping round like a grasshopper, "I can't keep it hot any longer without it drying up, Ted", she wailed. "Ada, calm down and lets get on with it. Come on we wunna wait any longer. Looks like pub comes before wife and family." So Ted carved up the bird, hoping it would feed all or them, it was the biggest he could buy at the last minute. They all said grace and Ada dished up a right royal feast. No one missed big Jim but they did miss young Jim. Ted sat in his place and Ada took up Sal's chair. Everyone was having a good time, all wishing it could go on forever, the young ones eyes sparkled and their laughter filled the house. Upstairs Sal listened to them and tears welled up in her eyes. This was the first Christmas she hadn't sat down with them, it wasn't like Jim to let them shout and carry on like this, he must have turned over a new leaf she thought. Ada came up with a small plate of dinner for her, she hadn't much appetite but she didn't want to upset Ada. "Is everythin' alreet Ada?" she enquired. "Well um", she stammered, not wanting to upset Sal. "Ada, what's up, ye'd best let on." "Oh well, its just Jim hasn't come back from t'pub yet." she stammered "So we couldn't wait no longer, Sal, hope that's all right with thee." "Aye Ada, its alreet, dunna botha a leopard never changes its spots," she laughed. Ada could see she was agitated, but she had to go and dish up the pudding. "Now our Sal, just you get that down thee and dunna fret, we'll have yer on yer feet in no time at all."

The kids were waiting for their pudding, there were a couple of three-penny pieces in it. So, who would be the lucky ones, a big jug of custard was steaming on the table, everyone had lashings and soon they were all full to burstin'. Ted had found a three-penny piece in his puddin' so he gave it to Lizzie and he made sure that Alex and Teddy had one each too. Jean gave hers to Joe so they were all happy. Ada was amazed that four children had a three-penny piece each when she had only put two in the puddin.

Ada then asked Ted to take the kids round to their house just in case Jim came home with a skin full. Ted was disgusted at him, couldn't understand a man putting the pub before kith and kin, he was glad to get home to his own house, he could relax now in his armchair. No comfort round at Sal's place. Camy was sent round too so she could play with the young ones and Ted could have his after dinner nap.

Ada, Jean and Mary tackled the mountain of dishes, there'd never been so much tooing and froing, with water from the fireplace and the stove they had nearly finished when Jim staggered through the back door. "Merry Chishmush", he slurred, trying not to laugh, the look on Ada's face was a bloody picture. "Hast saved any dinner fa me?" he asked. Ada pointed to the oven, not wanting to speak to this bloody reptile. He opened the oven door took one look at the dried up dinner, banged the door shut again and thought, "fuck this lot, I'm off to Meg's, she'll make me some dinner and she'll warm me up in bed!" So he turned and walked out again, "Sod the bloody lot of them let em all piss off" he staggered off down the street. A few curtains were lifted up and tongues were wagging. He could imagine it, "poor old Sal, married to such a rotter." He laughed out loud, ner mind eh, sod em all. Sal would be better off without him. Thinking of Sal sobered him up a little bit, it was no good thinkin' of her, no good at all, he'd thought of her for twenty bloody years, where had it got 'im, no bloody where, that's where.

Back at the house, Ada was brisling with indignation, the swine the bloody drunken swine, how could he behave like this with Sal so poorly upstairs. "She musn't be told," she said to Mary, Jean and Harry. "Dunna say owt to yer mam, she must have peace and quiet at all costs." Ada brewed up and lumbered up the narrow staircase with a cup of tea for her poor sister married to a good for nothing drunkard. She wiped the tears from her eyes and put on a big grin for Sal's sake. "Eh by gum, our Sal, we're all bloody nye bustin' out at seams." she said twirling round to show off her ample curves. Sal had to giggle, she couldn't help it. Jim would call her the fat bastard but it was funny to see her in full flow. "Did Jim enjoy his dinna'." she asked. Ada bustled round not meeting her gaze, "Oh 'e cleared 'is plate and is snorin' by 't fireside now." she lied. "Now lady you get some rest here's yer tablet and water and after you've sipped yer tea get some sleep." Harry came bounding up the stairs with Ted's old walking stick, "her mam, this is to bang on the ceiling wi' if thee wants owt." Ada scolded Sal, "dunna yer go knockin' every five bloody minute nar, da yer err, or we'll whack yer wi it, won't we Harry." He looked at his mam and said quietly "I wouldn't harm a hair on her head Aunty Ada." Sal and Ada filled up with tears. "Yer great soppy apeth," Sal wiped her eyes with the back of her hand. "I don't deserve any of 'em Ada. I've not been a very good mother." Ada stopped her in full flight. "No then our Sal, I'll have none of that crap. What you want is a good sleep, so down yer get and no mither or I'll want to know the reason why." She plodded back down the stairs, thankfully Harry hadn't said owt about his Dad's shenanigans. She felt afraid of what the night would bring, perhaps he would sleep on the settle and not disturb Sal, she could only hope. What will Ted say when I tell im about Jim, she wondered, thank God for her Ted, she swallowed hard at the lump in her throat. Must get on with the jobs, keep busy, don't think about him.

Young Jim came to the door, "is it safe to come in Aunty Ada?" he asked, "Oh I Jim" Ada was pleased to see him, "Nip up now and see yer mam before she gets off to sleep." she urged. Jim flew up the stairs and Ada thanked the Lord for sending young Jim round. She was in need of young Jim. She would tell him about his Dad and ask his advise about what she should do. Young Jim stayed with Sal for about ten minutes. "She's nearly asleep Aunty Ada, she said it were the tablet she'd taken. Anyway she looks better today dunna yer think Aunty Ada?" "Aye lad, she does and we want her to stay that way, so dunna let on that yer Dad didn't have his dinner today, Jim. He came home absolutely sozzled, couldn't hardly bloody stand up, slammed the oven door and sodded off without a bloody word." Me and Ted had slogged our bloody guttsies out getting dinna', "What yer think of that our Jim?" "Well" said Jim "I canna say I'm surprised knowing 'im. Eh but its rotten fer you Aunty Ada, he's a rotten bugger, all is as bin, we all know it, there's nowt we can do about it, only hope he falls down a stinkin' sewer or summat." She could see he had his fists clenched tight at his sides. Eh, by eck, that man would get his come uppance one day. When young Jim was a bit bigger and stronger. "Ner mind lad, dunna fret, come on we'll 'ave a nice cuppa tea, then you get off and tell uncle Ted to bring the kids round for bed soon. "Dunna tell 'im about yer Dad. The kids have enough to worry about without owt else. Jean and Mary went out for the night, bless 'em, they were good lasses and had been a right good help to Ada. She was just about buggered, what a bloody life, no kids of me own and now I've got nine and their mother to see to. She was a good old soul was Ada Harris and everyone loved her so.

Well by the time Ted had bought the kids round they were almost asleep on their feet. Camy put them to bed and sat down with Ada and Ted. They were talking about Jim, wondering what to do about him that night. Camy was very calm, "he'll be OK Aunty Ada, he's always too drunk to shout and rage, he goes right up to bed and sleep right away mam always says." "Well all we can do is hope so." They sat and waited for Jim to return the girls and Harry had all come home and gone to bed, Sal was sleeping peacefully and Ted and Ada had almost nodded off when Jim came home. He was looking a bit sheepish, he hadn't had much to drink since dinner time, he had been in bed with Meg most of the afternoon and evening and he was reasonable happy. The sight of Ted and Ada waiting up for the naughty boy almost made him laugh out loud. "Sorry about dinna', Ted" he said keeping his head down and feeling foolish. "Nay yer mind Jim, its Christmas after all." said Ted. Ada glared at him, bloody gutless men was what she said to herself. "Right we're off" she barked "Our Sal's sleepin' nar, dunna wake her." "I'll be sleepin' on't settle tonight," said Jim "Dunna want to disturb her, best let her get her rest." "Christ Almighty" said Ada when they were outside the house, "he canna be tryin', can he Ted, sorry for what he's done, I dunna belief it, well, well, well!"

From that night Jim was a better man, not a good father and husband but he didn't come home drunk so often, he still went out every night to see Meg and Ginny, but he was a lot calmer and the kids were glad of that. Things carried on much the same, Sal got stronger every day and in a couple of months she was on her feet and almost her old self. Jim's wedding was getting closer, so she had been sewing while she was confined to bed and she had made the most beautiful pillow slips and tablecloth, embroidered with birds and flowers and little love hearts. She was very pleased with her work and couldn't wait to show it off.

On new years day, 1935, Jim told her he was never going to have marital relations with her again, she had been glad of this and thanked God. She would get better now, she knew, without all that animal grunting and fumbling, she could do without all of that. She wouldn't miss any o' that, not ever. She knew he would be doing it with some other woman but she didn't care as long as it wasn't her.

By the time of Jim and Tilly's wedding, Saturday 24th August, Ada had bought clothes from the jumble sales for the kids and Harry, Jean and Camy had made dresses for themselves with Ada and Sal's help. It was a lovely day and Tilly looked radiant. Everyone was happy, only the absence of Jim's father spoiled the day, it was very embarrassing for young Jim but he wasn't unduly bothered, he knew his father was trying to sort himself out, but was too stubborn to ever say he was sorry. Tilly would have been right with him, but young Jim would rather spit in his eye. Sal was looking better and really enjoyed herself. The Bennett's had put on a nice wedding feast and the kids never stopped eating.

Everybody had to agree, poor they might be and many in number, but they all had very good manners and could be taken anywhere without fear of being shown up.

So the year progressed with everyone getting on with their lives and before long Jean told the family she would be getting married to Tilly's brother, Arthur Bennett. The wedding was set for Saturday 4th April, 1936, so everyone started up with their sewing and saving. Fancy two brothers and sisters marrying like that said the neighbours. Jean wanted Mary, Camy and Lizzie to be her bridesmaids and they were all so thrilled they could speak of nothing else for weeks. Ada and Ted travelled to Nottingham and bought a roll of cloth, enough to make all the dresses. They sewed and sewed from morning 'til night enjoying every moment.

Camy surprised herself by becoming a very able weaver, it had suddenly become easy to her and she handled the looms like a good 'un. She was taken off the learners corner and given her own four looms. She was so proud she would show everyone how good she could be. I'll be looking after eight looms in a couple of months, she vowed. She had got the hang of the weavers knot at last and it couldn't be broken. She sang from morning 'till night. no one could hear her and it helped pass the time a little bit. Most of the factory lads had tried their hand with her, but she wouldn't go out with any off them. Sister Mary was courting strong and Harry too, he was in love with Peggy Barlow, she was a weaver too and Camy liked her, she loved Harry and wanted to talk about him all the time. They would have a chat at break times. She sometimes asked Camy why she would not go out with any of the lads. Camy said she would know the one for her as soon as she saw him and no one else would do. Everyone would laugh thinking she was playing hard to get, but she meant every word.

Before they knew where they were Christmas was upon them again and then 1936 was in full swing. Big Jim was better behaved towards his family but no one dared mention weddings to him or he would go berserk. They realised that we would not be attending any, so young Jim would be giving away the bride in his father's place. Everyone had a splendid time and while young Jim was making his speak he announced that Tilly was having a baby. It was due in September, everyone clapped their hands and Jim and Tilly had faces as red as beetroots. "How dost they feel about bein' a granny then Sal?" asked Ada. Sal didn't quite know she said it hadn't properly registered yet. What would big Jim say, him a granddad, he wouldn't be best pleased. Jean looked radiant and everyone said she was a lovely looking girl, as the whole family was. Very good features they had.

September came, hot and dry. On the 24th September, Tilly went into labour, she had a very bad time of it, she cried and screamed for hours and Jim was beside himself with worry. "She's goin' ta die," he cried "what can we do?", go for a walk urged the women-folk and when you get back it will all be over. He decided to go to the cottage they were getting ready to move into, it needed a lot of work, but he had a lot of helpers, so it wouldn't take too long before they could be in and on there own. He had got fed up with trying to stop the bed from creaking every time they made love, which seemed to be every night. They just couldn't get enough of one another, but he would feel embarrassed the next morning sitting opposite Mr. and Mrs. Bennett, when they asked if he had slept well.

One of Mr. Bennett's brothers had died leaving the cottage empty so it had been easy to get it for Tilly and himself. The rent was small so it would be champion. He scraped the paper off a couple of walls and swept up, made himself a brew of tea and worried about Tilly. Would she still be alive, he darn't go back, he couldn't live without her. "Oh Tilly, why did you want a baby, we could have bin just as happy on our own.

Jean and Arthur came looking for him, he had been gone for six hours. He was sat with his head in his hands. "Jim", they shouted, "Jim, come on home, the baby's arrived." "Is Tilly still alive?" groaned Jim. "Course she is, ya fat 'ed, come and see your little girl." "A girl?" said Jim, "but its got to be a boy." said Jim "Well we're sorry lad, but you'll have to have another then, cos its a girl." said Arthur. "Oh, I'm sorry Arthur, I didn't mean owt by it, as long as Tilly and the baby are alreet I dunna care."

Tilly was sat up in bed with their baby in her arms, Jim dashed to her holding her close. "Tilly, my love." he cried. "I've bin so worried, was it bad for yer?" Tilly said she had suffered the most terrible pain she had ever known, but it had all been worthwhile. She pulled back the shawl, and there was his little girl, tiny and pink, "she looks like mam." he exclaimed. "Do you think so?" he asked Tilly, "yes I think she does a bit," said Tilly. "Do you want us to call her Sally?" "Eh yes lass, that would be really nice, How about Sally Victoria." said Jim "Tilly, that's really lovely Sally Victoria Moore." Everyone agreed that it was a really nice name and Sal was overcome with emotion. She didn't deserve their love, but they gave it without a thought, she was really blessed, she knew that.

CHAPTER

9

Camy was doing very well at the mill, she now had eight looms of her own and was as skilled as anyone else, much better than some she had her bad days when everything seemed to go wrong but on the whole she did very well. Mr. Entwistle used to say good morning to her every day. He only spoke to his best weavers the others he turned away from. Camy was proud of her skills and punctuality, although she couldn't afford to let things go wrong, if she had a mess, she didn't want to pay someone to help her to unweave, which you had to and paying money out of your wages when it was badly needed was a sin, showed that you had not been vigilant, so it made for a more careful and industrious worker.

That night after work she walked down to the canal to see the barges in loading their cotton from the mill. Whole families lived on the long boats and it was fun to watch the kids and dogs and mam and Dad all giving a hand. It looked like a very hard life and she was glad she didn't have to do it. Aunty Ada had told her about her forefathers being barge dwellers and the life they led and of the tragedies that had happened now and then. A girl of about here own age was walking past her with two big containers, she said "hello" to Camy, " It's b'en a fine day," Camy answered back "what are you doin' wi them?" The lass told her she was going to the pub to fill them with drinking water. "Can I give yer a hand?" asked Camy. "Aye, thanks very much, her' yer are." she said handing over one of the containers, it was heavy without any water in. Bloody Hell, thought Camy, what's it like full up.

"What's yer name?" the girl asked . "I'm Cameo Moore" she answered giving her full title. "Cameo" the girl asked "Aye that's right Cameo Moore, everybody calls we Camy." she added. "Righto" the lass said "It is a posh name, I've never heard it afore." "What's yours," enquired Camy. "Well my names Aggie, short for Agnes, horrible isn't it?" It was really, but Camy didn't like to hurt the girls feelings, "eh, its not so bad really

Aggie, its alreet."

Camy ran home when they reached the corner, "I'm just goin' to tell me mam where I am, wait there," she said.

Sal was just getting ready to put out the evening meal, "mam is it alreet if I help lass from barges to carry some drinkin' water." she said breathlessly. "Aye but dunna be long or yer dinner will be in bin." Camy dashed out again and together she and Aggie went to the Goyt Inn. Mr. Jennings opened the door to them, "Hello, Miss Moore, whatever ye be after, ye father's not ere yet." "I'm just wi Aggie, Mr. Jennings." she told him, "I'm helpin' her with the water." "Righto, the taps there in the yard, 'elp yersens." He liked Camy, she was a lovely lass, the prettiest of all the Moore lassies. What a beauty she would be in another year or two.

They filled up the containers, shouted their thanks and headed back to the canal basin. The weight was terrific. Christ Almighty, what ever did she get bloody well have to get herself into this for, still if Aggie had to carry two containers what would it be like for her. They struggled on and at last after much stopping and starting they were there. Aggies' mother came to help them, she grinned and showed a row of brown rotten teeth. God, how awful, thought Camy, who's own were like row of pearls. She was filthy dirty, but she was friendly enough. "Who's this, our Aggie?" she asked. "Oh, its Miss Cameo Moore." said Aggie. "By eck, that's a right posh name, Cameo," said Aggie's mam. "Everybody calls me Camy." she said, feelin daft. Me mam called me after a brooch. Well they laughed even louder, "After a brooch, What kind of brooch." asked Aggies mam. "A cameo brooch." she answered. "What's a cameo brooch, when its at 'ome?", "My mam always keeps it in her pocket." "Well lass, its a damn good job she didn't have a fag in her pocket or hankie or you'd have been name after them instead. Camy was fed up with being the but of her jokes, but she liked Aggie, so she let it slide. I'll have to go home now Aggie fer me tea." "Righto" said Aggie, "I'll look fer ya on Saturday, come fer a walk down canal." "I will that," said Camy and off she went. She was fair hungry and wanted her tea.

On Saturday afternoon when her chores were done she told Sal she was going for a walk with Aggie. "Take Alex and Lizzie." she was told, so off they all went. She stopped at the barge and asked for Aggie. "She's gone fer water," they said. Again, thought Camy, poor bugger, they turned to look for her and sure enough here she was laden down with the two big containers. Before much longer they set off along the canal footpath.

There was a young lad just ahead and when they were out of view of the barge he waited for them to catch up with him. "Hi ya Aggie." he said. "Oh Lenny," she blushed under the muck on her face. "mam doesn't like me taking to Lenny, but I like him ya see. You dunna mind if he walks wi us do ya?" Camy didn't mind, she was happy with Lizzie and Alex, they loved going for walks, the only problem was watching they didn't get too close to the canal water. Barges were passing up and down and now and again a rich deep baritone voice filled the air. They left the path and went through a field filled with buttercups and daisies, they set about making daisy chains and soon had lots of links around their necks. The little ones loved it and ran about until they were worn out. When the light began to fade they set off home. Aggies lad gave her a peck on the cheek, she was thrilled to bits and touched her face in delight.

She arranged to meet him on Sunday and asked Camy along. "I take the little ones to Sunday School," she told Aggie "then I have to help mam with the tea and ironing, ready for work and school on Monday." Aggie was disappointed, "Well I'll see yer agin in a few weeks, we go back on Monday mornin'." "Oh, I'll look for yer then Aggie, bye till then." and Aggie was gone, what a life she must have travelling about from place to place. I wouldn't mind it apart from being as black as chimney, she couldn't do with that, Camy was spotlessly clean, her clothes were well worn hand me downs, but clean as a new pin. When she went indoors with the kids mam's face was pulled and she snapped,

"Were the bloody hell have you been to all this time?". Camy didn't get time to answer. "Git tin bath out and bath these two, they're filthy. They weren't really filthy but you couldn't argue with her when she was in this frame of mind. Harry came in and told Camy the reason for mam's mood. He had told her he was getting married next year to Peggy, so that was another wage packet less she would be getting, and our Mary is thinkin' about it too, he said. Sorry Cam you always seen to get the shitty end of the stick. Try not to let it get you down, go and talk to Aunty Ada if it gets too much for yer.

Camy got on with her chores and then put the little ones to bed and read them a story. She went to bed herself just after. She wanted to be on her own. She missed Jim and Jean and now Mary and Harry, God it was awful, she cried herself to sleep. There'd be nobody left soon, the house would be quiet, like the grave. I wish I could find someone just for me then I wouldn't feel so lonely.

Sally Victoria was a little angel and Camy loved her. She would be taking her out in her bassinet tomorrow morning. Jim and Tilly were so happy in their little cottage, Dad hadn't spoken to them yet or seen little

Sally, but as Jim said it was his loss. He would be the one to regret it, not them. Camy wondered if Jean and Arthur would have any babies, she could look after them all. That way she wouldn't be lonely.

Christmas was upon them once again and Camy was singing her head off as usual. Her mouth was moving but no sound could be heard, only the clattering of the machinery. The new weft carrier was on his rounds trying his best to get in between the looms and not bang his hips on the moving parts. He was black and blue, it was like a bloody obstacle course. He was watching Camy, he wondered what she was singing, my but she was beautiful, his breath caught in his throat. She was the most beautiful girl he had ever seen. He dropped all the weft bins on the floor with a great bang and she looked across at him, their eyes met and held for what seemed like ages. Oh, my God, did you ever see such a great lookin' man, those eyes like deep pools, she felt herself going red in the face and turned quickly away, lest anyone noticed. You only had to look at someone twice in the shed and you were droppin' yer draws for em. He was deeply embarrassed to say the least, he quickly gathered up the tins, but didn't know which weft went into which tins. Jessie with eyes like a hawk went to his aid, "what the hell art doin' lad." she said, By God he was a handsome lad, those eyes, those beautiful big eyes, by gum, he was going to break a few bloody hearts as like as not. She helped him with the weft tins and he was gone. Camy's heart was still thumping, God Almighty, he was so handsome, thick dark hair, well shaped bones, tall about six foot two and by the look of his arms, strong too. What was someone like him doing here at the mill. She wanted to know his name and everything else she could about him. He must have a wife and probably kids, thought Camy. Her friend Nellie came to see her, "Hey Cam lass, hast seen new weft carrier," she shouted. "Aye, I have that Nellie, who is he dust know?" Well Jessie said he was Irish with a funny name, she couldn't say, he's living with his relatives somewhere round here. By eck, I'd give owt for a fella like him." she said and pretended to swoon and they both laughed. Camy felt strange, she couldn't understand it she had butterflies in her guts and she felt sick. She had to stay and do her job she would never be allowed to go home in the middle of day, so she got on with it, her eyes darting this way and that, looking for a head of dark curls. She though she spotted him a time or two then he was gone. She was so busy looking she put two shuttles in at the same time and what a bloody mess she had. This will cost an absolute fortune." she groaned as the two helpers came along. mam would go mad with her money being down next week. She was so engrossed, she didn't see him come back with the weft tins. By the time she realised he was walking away. She wouldn't look at me, he thought, maybe next time, he couldn't wait.

When they went home at five-thirty he was walking just behind her and he saw where she turned off to her house, that was well worth knowing. He caught up with one of the warehouse lads who asked him if he was goin' to the pub that night. He said he would maybe she would be there. Of cause she wasn't, Camy had ever taken to drink. She had seen what it had done to her father that was enough for one family.

Next day at the shed everyone was making merry, it was Christmas Eve and the men where chasing the lasses for a quick kiss, trying for a grope if they were lucky. Nellie came in with a bottle of sherry and they all had a swig, it was horrible but it made Camy feel very bold. She spotted the Irishman and couldn't believe her nerve, she marched up to him and said "Hello!" "Hello yourself," he answered in the sweetish Irish accent. Oh, her toes were curling up, "and who might you be," he said, "I'm Cameo Moore," she answered, "What's your name?" She was trying to speak nicely, didn't want to put him off. "I'm Finton O'Grady" he said "very please to meet you, Cameo." he said She was tongue-tied and ran back to her work feeling very foolish. At least she knew his name, Finton O'Grady, what a wonderful name, she said it to herself over and over again. She looked over to where she had left him, but he was gone. Will I see him again before the Christmas break was over, I hope so, he filled her mind all the rest of the day, she could think of nothing else.

It's a bloody good job you've finished today." said Jessie making her jump out of her skin, "yer fit for bugger all, fancy drinkin', yer'll be getting the bloody sack if Mr. Entwhistle sees yer. Camy didn't tell her it wasn't drink. She had only had one swig and it had worn off hours ago. Let her bloody well think what she wanted. Can't be bothered wi her. "Yer were a bit forward wit new lad weren't yer", Jessie asked, "bowling up to 'im like that, very brazen, if yer ask me." Camy wanted to shout at her "Well I'm not askin' thee, so bugger off," but she just said "I was only bein' polite to him, him bein' a stranger, Jessie, that's all. He was looking a bit lonely." "Aye lass I suppose so, just dunna yer get doin' owt daft cos its Christmas. I've seen many a one rue the bloody day, I'm tellin' yer." "Aye, Jessie, thanks very much, yer dunno after worry about me," Bloody hell she hadn't asked to look at his arse. What would the old cow say to that, "Piss off," she said under her breath. "Piss off, you old tart, bloody old sow, go and get yer knickers down fer ol' Wrighty, you ol' bag." She started to laugh to herself, thankful the old cow couldn't hear her. The hooter sounded for home time that was the end of work for a day or two.

she hoped she would get to see him over the Christmas holidays, if not she would be wishing each day away until she was back at work again.

There were pots to do and her night was spent helping mam now that Harry was married to Peggy Barlow and Mary married her Brian. Joe was thirteen now, nearly ready for work. Teddy was eleven, Lizzie nine and little Alex was seven. There was still plenty of work to be done at home. She would be eighteen next year on the 28th October. mam told her Jean had been round to see her, "she's expecting a baby in June," she said. "Oh, mam, that's nice," she said. Sal's expression was the same as always, sullen and miserable, "Oh, why couldn't she be happy for Jean, another baby to take out for walks in the bassinet. Camy was happy, she loved babies, she hoped she would have one or two one day. She thought about Finton O'Grady, babies with his dark hair and eyes with huge long lashes, she wanted to tell mam about him, but she knew mam wouldn't be interested. She never was, what a bloody carry on. She felt she had to tell someone, so when she had finished her jobs, she went round to see Aunty Ada. She was putting the finishing touches to the Christmas presents for the kids. Ada poured her a drink of Shandy, and she wished her a merry Christmas. "Oh, Aunty Ada Camy told her "there's a new weft carrier started today and he's absolutely wonderful. He's Irish, his names Finton O'Grady, his eyes are, Oh well, I don't know really. He's just the best looking man I've ever seen." Ada was watching Camy and she could see the lass was smittin'. She'd never mentioned a lad before, she was a pretty girl, the most striking of the family and when she let her hair loose, she was beautiful. "Well now, lass." said Ada, "just you be careful and think on do yer er." Oh, Aunty Ada, dunna be daft he's probably married with a couple of brats," they laughed, but Ada could see the laughter wasn't in her eyes.

Camy couldn't sleep that night she tossed and turned and thought of Finton, hoping he wasn't married or if not that he didn't have a steady girl.

When Christmas dinner was over and she had washed up and tidied for mam, she asked if she could go round to see Jim and Tilly and little Sally. Sal told her to be gone, dad was sleeping off his booze and dinner in the parlour. The kids were upstairs playing with their toys. It was a cold day, and it looked like it would snow again before the day was out. She walked round to Jim's little cottage, it was always so snug and warm there, they were so happy together. They were pleased to see her as always, she gave them a doll for little Sally, she had made it herself and clothes to change into. Little Sally can round the room with dolly, highly delighted.

Her golden curls bobbing about like strings. "Have yer seen our Jean?" she asked, "Ey lass, she called round last night. A baby in June, eh? some more knitting for they, eh lass?" Yes I think I'll get a pattern out and start tonight," laughed Camy. "Shall ye stay fer tea?" asked Tilly, "No I'd better not mam will want a hand with the kids, thanks all the same," said Camy. "I'd better be off," she gave them all a hug and kiss, it was nice to have a family, one you could hug and kiss.

She was walking up the street, back home when someone called her name, she turned and saw it was Finton O'Grady, "Oh God," she thought "what do I look like after playing with little Sally." He caught up with her and asked where she had been, she couldn't quite understand the Irish accent, so had to ask him twice what he had said. They laughed together and walked on by the time she reached home, she knew he was single and had come over from Ireland to stay with his Aunty Mary and her husband Uncle Paddy O'Reilly and their four kids. There was no work where he lived in Ireland and his folks were very poor, so he had set out to make his fortune. She could have listened to his sweet Irish accent forever, but she was home now and she didn't know what else to say. She could say come in and have a cup of tea, but her Dad wasn't like anyone else's Dad, he would hit the roof. "I'll see you again Finton," she said. "Oh call me Fin, everyone else does, well cheerio for now Cameo," he said and she turned and almost ran into the house. I'm in love, she said, to herself, I must be I'm going all ga-ga. He's not married, Oh thank you, Lord, thank you. She couldn't wait to get back to work wished Christmas was over.

It went quickly enough and she found herself back at the loom, just a few more days and it would be New Years Eve and 1938 would be here. What would it bring, she wondered. All morning long her eyes searched the floor for any sign of the weft carrier. Bessie with the one tooth signalled her over to her looms. "What's up wi thee," she asked Camy "you look like a startled fawn, at all reet?" Camy nodded "Aye course I am Bessie, is it that reet grandly lookin' Irish lad that yer looking fer?" she asked, her eyes twinkling, her one tooth wobbling up and down. "Dunna be soft." said Camy "I'll have to get back", and she shot off back to her looms and set about finding the broken thread. She was so engrossed she didn't see Fin take her weft tins. He tried to catch her eye but everyone was watching him like hawks, so he scuttled and was miles away before she realised , bloody hell, I've missed him, she thought. She'd waited all bleedin rotten stinkin mornin' and now she'd missed him. Camy felt like crying, she was so mad. She would have to find an excuse to see him for just a few minutes, she pretended she was short of weft and couldn't wait for the tins to come back, so she whistled to Bessie and asked, "Look after em for me I've run out o weft." Bessie gave her a knowing wink and turned to shout to Fanny next to her, "She's run out of weft Fanny." "You dunna bloody say." answered Fanny and they both burst out into peels of laughter. "Wants er bloody arse felt," said Bessie. "He can feel my arse anytime." Camy went scarlet in the face but bustled out of the shed into the warehouse.

All the men started to shout to her and whistled. God they were bloody awful, she hung her head and almost ran through, "Have a look at this Camy," someone shouted to her, "look at the length." They all started to laugh, deep vulgar laughter, she ignored them, it was best to do that with men it only made them worse when you answered them back. She was in the weft room, huge baskets with numbers gainst them. She looked for her's trying not to look around for Fin. Her heart was thumping in her breast, she started to fill her tin and had almost finished when she sensed someone behind her. She turned and looked into those deep pools called eyes. Her face turned crimson again, he held her gaze, "The top of the morning to you, Miss Cameo Moore." he said. "Oh hello, Fin," she said, trying not to show her feelings, " have you had a nice Christmas." Oh to be sure and be God wasn't it just about the best." he laughed, he was mocking her, she could see that, but not laughing at her. "and how about yourself, Oh, fine really, very busy you know." They stood looking at each other not knowing what to say next. "I'd better get back," she stammered., "Ta-ra" she bustled past him and he watched her go, why the hell didn't he say something, for the love of God, why didn't he ask her out, what the hell was wrong with him. He couldn't get her out of his mind, she haunted him night and day, yet as soon as he had the chance, he was like a bloody child, tongue-tied and stupid. Oh, Cameo, beautiful Cameo, how am I going to get to know you how would he get to kiss her luscious lips to hold her in his arms. "Come on lad, dunna stand there day dreaming." said Cyril his overseer, he jumped to it and Cyril started on about youth of today. How they were bloody bone idle, "you should have been around when I was a lad," he moaned "there wasn't time to stand about, bloody gawpin, get them bloody tins filled, I want a baccy." He was a miserable bugger was Cyril, his wife was a nag so he took it out on everybody else. She was pug ugly as well, which made it worse, an ugly old nag and she was his, Lord help him. He often wondered if she would die, no the old sod would probably live 'til she was a hundred years old, by eck, he wished he could have one of them youngsters he'd show em a thing or two. He went off the cludgy where he would think above the youngsters and masturbate, everyone knew about him, but he didn't know they knew. He was the laughing stock of the shed, there he goes again they'd titter to one another. Off to pull his string, dirty sad old bugger.

Camy raced back to her work, what a silly little bugger she was, why hadn't she said something, standing there looking bloody daft. She didn't deserve anything else. I had a chance there, she thought I did nowt about it. She told herself she would the next time if she got the chance. Bessie Shaw was waiting for her, "Come on lass, can't keep em all goin'." "Righto, Bessie, thanks," she said "Ta very much I'll do the same for you sometime." "Right, I'll go and have a fag then, won't be long." and off she went. Camy was so busy with all the looms to look after, she didn't see Finton bring back the weft, she only noticed it when Bessie returned and she went back to her own looms. She looked up and down but he was nowhere to be seen. I've done bloody well today, missed him twice I can't believe it, she felt like crying, what was the matter with her. Finton on the other hand could only think that she was ignoring him, twice in one day it couldn't be coincidence. What would he have to do, ask the bloody little people for help, if he was back home in Balymahinch he would do just that. He decided to wait for her at five-thirty and he wasn't going to be ignored not a third time. He was an Irish-man and knew his mind, he would not be cast aside no not now, not ever. I'll woo her with my wonderful Irish charm, he laughed to himself. So at five thirty-five he was waiting at the top of the mill yard and her she was looking his way. What was he going to say to her, his mind went a blank, he just stared at her like a fool. "What's up with thee," she said "you look half right," she hadn't meant to say that but it just came out, "I mean er, " "Oh, Its alreet Miss Moore, I know I'm half right it's in the family," he was smiling so she knew it was OK. "And have you been ignoring me the day?" he asked, his eyes searching her face, holding here eyes with his, "Oh, No," she answered breathlessly, trying not to let her eye's show what her heart was thinking, "I was so busy I didn't see thee." "Well I don't rightly know about that Miss Cameo", he chided, "Oh, don't keep saying that Finton," she asked "everybody calls me Camy, Cameo sounds a bit too posh." "Oh no it doesn't, Cameo is a beautiful name and I shall call you nothing else, to be sure." "Well I'll be going now mam will be waiting for me." "Can't you stop awhile?" he asked . "No, sorry but mam hasn't been very well and she needs my help." Will you be coming out later on?" he asked "no, not tonight" said Camy, " It gets very dark so I stay home and help mam get ready for New Year's Day. "Do you go to the dance New Year's eve?" he asked her desperately, "I've never been before, I can ask me mam." she answered." "Try Cameo, please try." he looked her in the eyes again and her knees almost buckled. He had the most beautiful eyes she had ever seen, dark pool, she called them, deep dark pools you could drown in. "I'll try Finton," she promised, "I'll try, ta-ra for now." "Good-bye, Cameo Moore, till we meet again," he bowed from the waist and she giggled and turned homeward but kept looking back, it was only then she realised she had been oblivious to everyone who must have passed them up the yard. "Hell fire, I'm goin' daft. Please God let me mam say yes to the dance on New Year's eve.

She ran home, rushing through the back door and slamming it shut behind her. The smile was soon wiped from her face as her Dad cam storming through from the parlour. "What the fuckin' ells goin' on." he screamed was it you, you bloody daft cow. He ran at Camy and got her by the hair, she squealed with fright and pain. "Don't you come into this bloody house like that again, this is not a bleedin doss house. He belted her across the head and face then threw her into the armchair, now you bleedin well think on lady, we all know yer only bloody half right in the 'ed. Now get on wi tea, your mam's in bed poorly, Don't bother her feed the kids and then try to clean the bleedin pig sty up and one wrong word and y'll get the back of my hand!" He went through the front door with enough noise to awake the dead. Camy picked herself up from the armchair and wondered what the hell had she done to deserve this. Her head was spinning and she looked into the wall mirror and saw the hand marks across her face, she began to weep, huge tears of anger and frustration. He always clouts me, he hates me what have I done to the bloody shitty bastard, he should bloody die, he wasn't fit to live. I bloody hate you Jim Moore she wanted to shout out loud and clear, but remembered mam was poorly. She finished off the tea for the others and tidied the house. Then she made a cup of tea and told Joe to watch the others which she went up to mam. Sal was sitting up in bed looking as pale as a ghost, she looked up at Camy. "What did he do to you Camy?" she asked, "Oh, nothing really mam," she wanted to cry, to see her mam hold our her arms and comfort her, but she never did, never kissed her better. Camy put it to the back of her mind, handing Sal her cup of tea. "What's the matter mam?" she asked. "Oh, just a dizzy spell, nowt to worry over, I'm just restin' up a bit. Will you do that bit of ironing for me before you go to bed?" "Right, mam, can I go't the dance, New Year's eve?" she asked "not daring to look her mam in the eye." "Dancing Camy? You want to dance, why'd yer want to go dancin'?" "Well" said Camy "I was talkin' to Nellie and the other girls at work, they said about it an I thought it would be nice." "I'm sorry Camy," said Sal "Yer'll have ta look after the kids fer me till I'm feelin' a bit better." She looked so poorly, that Camy dare not argue. "Righto then I'll get youngster to bed," she said and was out of the door like a flash, "can't go - Can't go - Can't go, I can't go and I won't see Finton and he'll find somebody else, she wanted to curl up and die. Why the bloody Hell is it always me. I'm knocked from pillar to post, nobody cares about me, nobody loves me, she began to weep again, great shuddering sobs racked her body. What the hell had she ever done wrong, mam didn't bloody care a shit, the thought of mam pale and ill upstairs made her stop and think what if mam was to die. People did, that would be worse, left with Dad, she was sorry for what she had thought, she must look after her mam, you only got one, she dried her eyes and went to get the kids undressed for bed. Joe was already doing just that, he was a good lad. "I've washed their hands Cam, and faces" he added. "I can see that Joe." looking at Alex and Lizzie with jam from ear to ear, she smiled and sent to the sink for the face cloth. She wiped over the faces of her two little angels and made sure they had their night shirts on. "Will you tell me a story, Cam?" asked Alex, and me said Lizzie, "Just one, Where's Teddy?" She asked Joe. "Just gone up." he answered. "Alreet you two," she answered, "just one it is, I've got a great pile of ironing to do, put the iron on the fire for me Joe before you go to bed" she shouted half way up the stairs. Two hours later she was still ironing. There might be less of them at home now but the ironing pile never seemed to get any smaller. It was after eleven o'clock and she had just finished and was putting the clothes away in neat piles when Jim came home. He was the worse for wear, he glared at her as though she was a dog. "Shift this load of shit you," he ranted She was always afraid of him when he had been drinking, his eyes were always wild, she moved the ironing and went up stairs out of his way. She got undressed and got into bed, she slept alone now Lizzie had her own bed now that Jean and Mary were gone, and Alex was too old to run and snuggle up to her now She missed them. One day she would have some kids of her own, me and Finton, she hoped with all her heart, wondering what their children would look like How it would be in their cosy cottage without a care in the world. She imagined them with a boy and girl or two girls or two boys perhaps or maybe twins. They would all have dark hair and eyes just like there father, he would be kind and gentle, not like him downstairs. My Finton will be the most wonderful lover in the whole wide world, he'll never shout and rant and rave and he would never ever tell her to fuck off not her kind and gently Finton, she slept the sleep of angels and awoke to a new day.

New Year Eve she couldn't wait to get to work and see him and see what he would say about the dance. Please don't go without me, she wanted to say, but she knew she never would. She might have dreamt about him, but in reality he was almost a stranger. She was putting out the porridge oats for their breakfast when Jim came downstairs. "You can forget work today, yer mam's too poorly to be left alone so get down't shed and tell that bastard Entwhistle you can't work today."

Camy's heart sank, she wouldn't see Finton, "No," she shouted she hadn't meant to do it out loud, it just came out. What did you bloody say yer little git," he started towards her "I didn't mean, no Dad, I just meant what'll I say to Mr. Entwhistle," "Tell the big footed bastard you won't bloody well be in today, get it, you daft cow? What do I have to bloody do to get it into that thick bleedin skull." She left the breakfast table, grabbed her coat and sent quietly out the back door.

She ran down the shed yard it was slippery under foot and she almost came a cropper. It was dark too the lamplighter had only just started to light all the lamps around. What a spooky place the shed was in the dark with no one around. The office was locked, so she went to the door nearest the warehouse, some of the men were already there. They looked at her "Yer a bit early lass, what's up has't pee'd bed?" "What time does the Boss come in?" she asked "Oh, he won't be in yet for another hour at least, what do yer want him fer?" said a kindly man. "Well I can't come in today, me mam's poorly, so what do I do now?" "Well, give me yer name and everything an I'll see he gets message." said the man. So Camy left word with him for Mr. Entwhistle and ran back home as fast as she could. Joe and Teddy were helping Lizzie and Alex to get ready for school, its a bit early for you yet" said Camy, "Dad told us to get ready, so we didn't argue." said Teddy in his matter of fact way. "Right, eat yer porridge up then and I'll see if mam wants a cup of tea. She was halfway up the stairs when Dad came down, he barged past her almost knocking her down the length of the stairs, "Get out of bloody way fer Christ's sake," he bellowed at her. "That ones not a full shilling." he muttered to himself. mam was trying to sleep, she'd tossed and turned all night and now she was tired out, "do yer want a cup a tea, mam?" Camy whispered. "No thanks, I'd just like to get some sleep, bring me a cup about half past ten lass." "OK mam." She shut the bedroom door quietly and hoped her Dad would be off to work before she got downstairs. He was waiting for her, "Right lady, you do everything yer mam tells yer, no bloody cheek mind, do yer hear me." "Yes Dad." she answered meekly, "Piss off you bloody bastard." she thought. He would kill her if she had said it out loud A few minutes later he was gone and she felt a load had been lifted off her shoulders. Right lets get on with it, she said and laughed with the kids about the big bad bear. After the kids had gone to school, she did the washing up and polishing through the house, she was in the parlour black-leading the grate thinking of Finton when Ada came through, she jumped out of her skin, "Oh, Aunty Ada you fair made we jump," "What the hell ar't doin' at home, Camy?" asked Ada, "Is our Sal alreet?" "She's not feelin' well Aunty Ada, Dad said I was to stay home." Camy told her. "Well you've done a grand job," she said looking round at the tidy home, poor but clean and bright. "Right, lass, I'll go up see how she is. Will yer make us a brew an bring it up?" Ada smiled at Camy. She was a good help this lass was and it wasn't easy for her. She knew that, she saw how Jim passed scorn onto the lass, perhaps because she looked so much like Sal, thought Ada. She lumbered up the stairs and went into Sal's room. "By eck, what a lazy bugger we are 'ere," she said sailing past the window and opening the curtains. "It'll be night-time soon our Sal." Sal turned over in the bed, she had been dreaming of William and now her dream was shattered, "Bloody Hell, Ada, is there no peace fer't wicked?" she asked. "No there isna, so come on sit up lets have a look at thee," she was still pale and thin and she always looked ill so Ada couldn't tell if she was worse or not. One thing she did know, Sal wasn't one to lie in bed in the daytime, so she must be poorly. "Do yer want I should get doctor, Sal?" she enquired. "Na our Ada, I'll be alreet, I just want a bit of quiet, some peace, yer knows. Lets have a fag ey." "We'll have one when Camy brings the tea." said Ada, plumping up Sal's pillows and reaching for her clean night dress.

"Ted's mythering me to bloody death ." she said "over Chamberlain, I told him, I'm not paid to run the country, he is, so let him get on wi it." "By eck, Ada Ted's always worried about government there's nowt he can do about it, whatever 'appens they'll do as they want, they wunna ask us owt" they both laughed at this. Poor old Ted wringing his hands and moanin'. He's moaned about Ramsey MacDonald then Baldwin then MacDonald again and now it was Chamberlain, who next, they wondered.

Camy bought up the tea and they lit up their fags, it was nice two sisters so fond of each other. One short and fat with a large red face and the other pale and thin and extremely attractive, in spite of everything. Her long hair shone and glistened in the pale winter light. "You won't feel like celebrating tonight Sal." said Ada "Shall I take young'ns to our house for't night?" "No, it's alreet Ada, I've asked Camy to see to them for me." "Well I'll give em the tea, they like tea wi Uncle Ted, it'll stop him from worrying about Chamberlain." They both tittered again about poor old Ted. "Righto, Ada will yer get me tablets off doctor the same as before, but dunna ask him to call. I'm alreet. Are yer listening to me." Ada smiled, "Yes alreet Sal dunna flap, I'll get thee pills an I'll call wi them at teatime when I call fer the children." They kissed each other fondly and Ada left Sal to rest. "Right," said Ada to Camy "I'm goin' ter shops and fetch yer mam's pills from the doctors, I'll take youngsters fer tea, are you comin' round as well?" "No thanks Aunty Ada I'd best stop wi mam eh." "Yes alreet Camy, I'll see yer later, ta-ra."

Camy was left to think about what might have been, the dance to-night, she couldn't bear to think about it, so she cleaned the brass and everything else that wasn't nailed down. There was a knock at the back door, she opened it to see their next door neighbour Mrs. Hibbert standing there. "I've bought thee mam some beef tea," she said and handed the basin to Camy, "see she drinks some now whilst its hot, think on lass." "Thanks, Mrs ." said Camy "I'll take it up to her now," Mrs. Hibbert was a nice old lady, she didn't neighbour, kept herself to herself, but if someone was poorly, she was always round with a bit of advice or some nourishment, Camy thanked her again and shut the door. Now what was she to do, mam would never touch anything she or Ada hadn't made or cooked. Poor they might be but mam wouldn't accept charity as she called it, but when it was a neighbour or friend you had to be very careful and not offend so the beef broth would be poured down the sink. She ran upstairs to tell Sal about it first of all. Sal pretended to be sick, "Bloody Hell lass throw the bugger away and thank her very much mind and tell her it's brought me back from the brink of death." They both laughed at this, "mam you are daft sometimes," said Camy, "mam?" she asked "Can I go round to our Jim's an see little Sally later on after tea. Sal thought about it and said she might as well the kids were goin' to Ada's fer tea, just make yer Dads and then go round. Are you calling on our Jean or Mary?" "NO, mam but I thought I might pop in and see Harry and Peggy just fer a few minutes, is that alreet." "Aye that's fine," said Sal "tell Jim and Tilly to bring Sally Victoria to see me tomorrow when they fathers gone out, alreet."

This was arranged and Camy was beside herself, she would have to pass by the hall where the dance was being held. At least she would have a chance to see him, only a slim one, but one she had to take.

Well today Friday 31st December was the last day of the year 1937 , what had 1938 in store for her, she could sense it was going to be a year never to be forgotten. Will it be the year I'm a bride, who will give me away, Jim, Harry? She would have to choose one day, but not yet. She washed her hair and rinsed it in vinegar to make it shine. It shone like silk, it had never been brushed so much. She pulled it up and pinned it, she didn't want her Dad to think she was up to anything or else she would be sent of to bed instead of scouring the streets for Finton O'Grady. Anyway her Dad came home from work and ate his tea in silence. All alone at the table, he liked it better like this without the kids, he couldn't stand any off the bastards, the whole bloody lot of them. He washed and shaved in the kitchen and Camy kept out of his way, pretending to be doing odd jobs about the house. He had enjoyed the tripe and onions and he was looking forward to a good New Year's Eve with Meg and Ginny. He climbed the stairs to get changed into his best suit, Sal was propped up in bed and she watched him change in silence. Neither spoke to each other, she knew about his women, she didn't mind it meant he left her alone. No more pawing and panting about and grunting and groaning, no more pain. She shuddered at the memory of the many times he'd taken her from behind. He was a well endowed man and when he was tanked up with drink and his lust for her was strong he put her through hell. He had said to her many times in drink, if you would just give yourself to me you would enjoy it, but she used to steel herself and make damned sure she didn't. He'd take one look at her gritted teeth and face a mask of suffering and thrust himself harder and harder into her and dig his fingers into her flesh and hurt her as hard as he could, hearing her wince with pain, spurred him on to greater heights. Now it was finished, over with once and for all, she wondered about his tarts. They would be drinking pals too, no doubt. Thick with make-up and the cheap perfume he reeked with night after night. Anyway they were doing her a favour so why bother. Jim caught her sneering gaze. "What the bloody Hell are yer lookin' at me fer", he shouted at her, she jumped, "I wasn't" she said, "I had a pain," she looked away. "I know you were fuckin' well staring at me and lookin' down yer bloody nose, just watch it you idle bitch or else," he shouted at her. She looked so scared so pale and thin, he didn't want to shout but he couldn't help himself. He could imagine what she would be like if he ever showed any love for her. He shook his fist at her and stamped off out of the bedroom and down the stairs. "Happy bloody New Year, Sal" she said.

Twenty five years ago she was with her William, it seemed like yesterday, she wished it were tomorrow, the door slammed downstairs and she knew he was gone, good bloody riddance, don't come back, you big bully. That what he was a big bully, in his prime Jim Moore was at his best hitting women and kids. He'd never set eyes on his grand-daughter, Sally Victoria, she was fifteen months old now and she was a little beauty, everyone said she looked like Sal. She couldn't see it herself, she was always happy to see Sally, but she knew what would happen to anything that she loved, they would be snatched away forever, so she didn't want to get too close like the rest of them did. Her chest was hurting, she didn't feel well. So she took two of the pills Ada had picked up from Doctor Hallam's for her. She soon began to feel drowsy. Camy came up to tell her she was off out, "I won't be long mam," "I'll be alreet, don't hurry back, I'm goin' to ave a sleep now."

Camy called round to see Aunty Ada and told her of her plans for the evening. Ada was taking the kids back round so she would be there for Sal, that made Camy feel easier and she could take her time now. "Be back about half past nine lass, then I can get home. I want to be up early to see to the turkey dinner, I don't think yer mam's going to be able to cope with it all. Bye, see yer soon then." "OK Aunty Ada" she said "I'll be back, ta-ra."

"I'm out, freedom" she sang to herself, at last she let her hair down and let it swing round her shoulders, hoping it looked alreet . It was like a halo round her face, she wished that she was allowed to wear make-up, just a bit would be nice, she didn't need it, but she couldn't know that. AS she turned the corner of the high street she heard the strains of the lovely new Gershwin tune, 'Love walked right in'. Someone was singing and it sounded really lovely, she sang along and swayed her body to the rhythm. Her eyes strained for a sight of Finton and although she waited for over ten minutes, not a sign of him was seen. She went to her bother Jim's house. Mustn't be too late or she would be too late to see Sally Victoria before she went to bed.

They greeted her warmly at the door and pulled her inside into the warmth out of the cold night air. Sally Victoria screeched with delight to see Camy, her very favourite Aunty. They hugged and played around and kissed fondly, they talked and played around for an house, then it was time for Sally to go to bed. Camy wished her a happy New Year and the little one answered back with a 'napa lees' which made them all laugh. While Tilly was upstairs, Jim poured Camy a glass of sherry. "It's only cheap stuff Cam, but better than nothin'," he said. "Its very nice, our Jim". said Camy. It was very sweet and made her feel all warm inside. "How's everything at home wi mam?" he asked her, "Well Dad's out every night as usual, mam's in bed again and I couldn't go to the dance tonight, sorry Jim, I didn't mean for it to sound like that, It's just that I wanted to go wi Nellie." "Poor Camy," said Jim "you're nearly eighteen and you never go anywhere, poor old girl. You'll have to stand your ground like the rest on us did or they'll never let you out of their sights." " Anyway, why dids't want to go to the dance, have you got your eye on some poor bugger then," she went bright red, "No I haven't our Jim, shut up." She finished off her drink and reached for her coat, " I'll have to be goin' now Jim, I promised mam I'd be back for nine-thirty." "See," he said "told thee dunna be late, hurry up 'ome, they'll have no life of they own, nar think on what I said, our Cam and dunna be such a little door-mat." "Happy New Year, Jim say ta-ra to Tilly for me." "Same to they, lass, hurry 'ome, he teased her."

She scurried down the street until she was approaching the dance hall again, lots of people were going in and some where standing about waiting for their partners. Her heart skipped a beat, was that Finton? No it was a stranger, her eyes searched in vain for any sign of the Irish-man. There was none. The band started up with the Bing Crosby's "Harbour Lights", she had been singing this for quite a while at work and she loved it, the singer wasn't up to much, but he didn't sing it badly, she sang along quietly to herself scanning the crowds again, always wishing it was Finton, there but he was probably with someone else by now, she felt tears sting her eyes and a lump the size of an egg was trying to choke her. She swallowed hard and turned for home, the two hall clock chimed half past nine. Better get back to mam, Jim's words were in her mind. Stand up for yourself, lass, don't be a doormat. Well that is what she had become, no dance for her, no bloody fun, what a shit life it was. She wouldn't see him now until work resumed on Monday morning. How can I exist until then, bloody families, she moaned. Let Monday come quickly, please God, just for me.

Ada was waiting for her on her return, "Yer late lass," she scolded. "Sorry, Aunty Ada, I had a glass of sherry with our Jim." Ada smiled, "sherry indeed, I think I'll have one with your Uncle Ted, Happy New Year love." she said. "Happy New Year, Aunty Ada." said Camy and they hugged each other. Ada looked down on her young niece, your a good lass our Camy. I know it's hard on yer, but It's worth it, for thee mam's sake isn't it." "Aye, Aunty Ada, dunna worry, I dunna mind none, I'll see yer in't mornin'." they said goodnight.

The kids were all in bed so she went up to see if mam wanted anything. She was drugged up with her pills, good thing they were, she wished she could swallow a pill and just sleep and forget everything. What a way to spend a New Year's Eve, all alone no one to share a joke with or a drink, a bit of fun a laugh or two. She wanted to cry again, but wouldn't let herself. I'm always crying she thought. Aunty Ada was right, she always said my bladder was stitched to me eyes. She decided to peel the spuds and veg for tomorrow, that would be one job less in the mornin', then I can have a bit of a lie-in. So the veg were prepared and meat was ready for the oven. She wondered if Ada had made a pudding, knowing her she would have left nothing 'til the last minute. It was almost midnight and she couldn't bare to stay up any longer, she wanted to sleep so that her thoughts of Finton would go out of her mind. As she went up the stairs holding her candle she had a beard of tears around her chin.

CHAPTER

10

Meanwhile Finton was in torment, Cameo had not been to work that day, he was unsure who to ask about her. All day long he looked around for her just in case she had overslept or something or would be in after the dinner break, but no, she didn't turn up. He didn't know her two sisters worked at the shed, they would have been able to tell him where she was. Every way he turned be became aware that the women-folk were watching him and the come hither glances he was getting made him very nervous. Why the hell couldn't she be there. Would she be at the New Year's dance tonight, yes sure she'd be there, he looked forward to that. God there was some sluts working here, most of them married too, he wasn't going to get involved with them, that was for sure. He'd got involved with his boss's wife back home in Ireland. He was working in the fields, gathering the hay bails when she came along with some bread and cheese and a pail of milk for him and she couldn't keep her hands off him. It was a hot summers day, she was a nymphomaniac and they were at it all afternoon and most of the night, he didn't really fancy her, but he couldn't resist her large ripe breasts, she was a big woman, not fat, big made, but by God, she knew every way and so did he by the time she had finished with him.

Anyway, her husband couldn't understand why she was missing half the day and night, he searched the fields and found them stark naked, except for the straw that was stuck to their arses. They were writhing and groaning so loud they never even heard him approach until it was too late. She screamed, Finton fled without his pants and all hell broke loose. He hid in another field until they had calmed down and went off with his clothes, then he followed them slowly, feeling bloody ridiculous. After waiting a while he ventured to the kitchen window where she was making tea, he tapped gently and she came outside, "Your clothes are in the outhouse," she said. "I'm sorry about himself, you'd better not be coming back. I'll have your pay sent on with one of the hands. He's threatened to shoot you on sight. My you're a darling boy," she said, looking him all over, she stroked him roughly, he backed away, "Oh, no you don't Mrs." he thought and he dashed off to find his clothes and was away with the wind. What would he tell his Ma and Dada, they would get to know soon enough. It was then that he decided to go to England. Bloody Hell, he had only had one woman and now look what had happened. He'd be shot on sight if he stayed there. He should have said no to the bloody woman, but how could you when your loins weren't listening, mind you parts of it had been good fun and he wasn't a virgin anymore. Nearly twenty-five and just had his first fuck, was all he could think off. He thought long and hard about it all later on that night and decided to wait until he found a really nice descent girl, one he could marry and have a family with. There were plenty of nice Irish girls living in England. He would find one for sure. So he set sail on an old tub a week later and said good-bye to his Ma and Dada and good-bye to his beloved Ballymahinch. Ma was beside herself, "I'll pray for you every day Finton, be sure and keep yourself safe from harm, my only child. It be sad we all are at your going, I'll ask father Flannigan to pray for you also God keep you safe my son, God bless you." He was glad to get away he couldn't stand the weeping and wailing. "I'll be back," he said. "Bye, take care." The rickety bus took him on the first leg of his journey, through Carrydoff and on and on until he reached Belfast Lough. There he sought out Captain Shamus McKeknie, he was sitting on an old bucket and he was sozzled. Finton waited with him until the crew helped him on board, he was a miserable old bugger, he snapped and snarled at them all. Finton sat on some old lagging on deck, this wasn't a package steamer, this was a rusty old tub. The crew were hoping to drop off a few crates of whisky contraband of course without the customs finding out. Well they weighed anchor and were of, it was getting dark by this time and he watched as the lights of Bangor came into view, further on he made out Donaghadee and then he couldn't tell anymore, he was lost then geography hadn't been his strong point at school. He watched until the twinkling lights were no more, "Good-bye, my Ireland, Good-bye my Homeland, God bless you until I'm back again." He wished he wasn't going to England, turn back, he wanted to shout, let me off, but everyone was busy rushing about no one wanted to know his needs. He wept quietly to himself, ma will she be alreet without me, would she die of a heartache like she had said every day this week. His guts suddenly felt peculiar, his head started to swim around, God Almighty he was sick over and over again. The sea got rougher and he was sicker, It never seemed to end. I'm going to die, he thought, he was dying and no one cared. Huge waves lashed the old tub, everyone shouted and ran about, no one took any heed of him, he wished he could shelter from the foul weather, he was soaked to the skin, covered in vomit, stank like a pole-cat, what else could happen? The ship could go down, he would drown, he retched again and again, but there nothing left to through up. He wanted to die, if he lived through this he promised himself, he would never sail again.

Land came into view, lights twinkled, we're there, thank God at last, he lurched up to one of the crew men, "That England?" he asked. "No," he answered, "that's the Isle of Man, Port Erin lighthouse." "How much further?" Finton asked, wondering how much longer he could go on like this. "Only another few hours." answered the crewman. Hours!, thought Finton, no, I can't stand it. The crewman bought him a mug of very strong sweet tea, it was awful but he felt a little better after he had got it down. He finally slept a little and awoke to a fine morning, the wind had dropped and the sea was calmer. One of the crew pointed his finger to leeward. Finton stood up, well tried, his legs buckled under him, he held on to the side and looked out, "Liverpool." shouted the man, "England." he grinned. Finton looked out at the wide expanse of land, so this was it. "What did England have in store for him, make it good, please God." he asked, "Let me be happy here." At last he was on English soil, he thanked Captain MrKeknee, the miserable old bugger was waiting for his money, "Come on lad, I've goods to deliver." thinking about his whisky and looking around for anyone suspicious. He could smell the Customs and Excise man a mile away. Finton paid up and was on his way.

Bootle, funny name, he thought. I'll find some where to stay and get cleaned up. He saw a bar 'The White Horse', so he went in and ordered half a pint of beer. The landlord was friendly enough, "Have you just come off the boat?", he smiled. "Sure and I have that, sir," he answered, "I won't be after crossing on one again for a very long time." He was still looking green and the landlord felt sorry for the lad, he was a tall handsome lad and thought he would be sure to be an asset to whoever he worked for, the lilting Irish accent was a bonus too. He struck up a conversation with the Irish lad and soon found out where he was headed, anyway the upshot was that Finton would work behind the bar for his keep and a couple of bob a week until he'd saved a bit more for his fare to Derbyshire. He could earn a bit more if he worked longer hours. This would give Stanley Meadows a bit more free time to spend with his wife, Winnie, who stayed on her own upstairs most of the time. She had gout,

"Too much port," Stan said, "but she won't stop drinking, so she has to suffer and so do I." he said, he was a good man and Finton was glad that he had called here. He would let his Uncle know that he would be staying here for a while, so it would give him time to try for the job at the mill for Finton.

So, here he was in Bootle, Liverpool and dreamed all night about the farmer's wife running around stark naked with a huge knife, trying to cut off his private parts. He awoke in a sweat a few times and vowed he would never dally with anyone else's wife again as long as he lived. The customers took to Finton, his easy way and the Irish blarney won them all over, he was popular with the ladies, but he was petrified to be left alone with any of them. Stan would pull his leg unmercifully about it, but Finton would never tell him the reason why. He didn't want Stan to think the worst of him, he'd think he was a gigolo and would boot him out and he wanted to stay, he liked it here. He loved the smell of the sea and walking around the harbour watching the fishing boats sailing in and seeing the catch unloaded and iced and boxed in a matter of minutes. He got to know one or two of the crew and there was always a few nice fish for him to take back to Stan and Winnie. They were very gratefully received by them , there was nothing nicer than a bit of fresh fish. Stan would do the cooking and Winnie would do the eating, she was very fat and ate from morning 'til night, but she had a heart of pure gold and Finton became very fond of her. She thought he was the handsomest male she had ever seen and those eyes, "Bye hell they will get you out of many a tight corner, and you'll never starve. I just wish I was twenty years younger, I'd give you a run for your money." Poor old Winnie too stupid to stop drinking and eating, she would kill herself with it one day but you couldn't tell her, she didn't want to know.

Trade was very brisk that summer and Finton worked hard for Stan and Winnie and didn't want to leave them but he knew his uncle was trying to get him work in Derbyshire, so he would eventually have to pack his bag and be off. So it was in late November, a note badly written from his uncle Paddy arrived, it was short and to the point. 'Have job, must start December 20th, Don't let me down, signed Uncle Paddy.' He bet his Aunty Mary had written it, Paddy couldn't write he was sure. Anyway he would have to go or there would be hell to pay.

He would have a couple more weeks with Stan and Winnie, then he would hitch a lift and try to save as much of his money as he could, he had just over ten pounds and he felt like a millionaire. That night he told Stan and Winnie about the job and they were sad, "You don't have to go,

Fin," said Stand "You're like a son to us, stay we won't see yer short." "Well I'm grateful for all you've done for me, both of you but I can't let family down, it isn't done, but if it doesn't work out, I'll come back if that's alreet. I might even be back with a wife and kids one day." he chuckled. They were sorry to see him go and Winnie cried, but the day dawned and he was off at half past seven in the morning. He had a lift from one of the locals as far as St.Helens. He hugged Stand and Winnie warmly, there were tears in Stan's eyes; he had grown to love the young Irishman like the son he had never had, he was very sad to see him go. He pressed some money into Fin's hand, "Take this," he said "keep it by you, it might come in handy." He wouldn't take no for an answer, so Fin was off and waved his last good bye.

The lorry was very old and it rattled and shook like it would fall to pieces, however he was glad of it and old Joe was a nice chap, didn't say much, but that wasn't a bad thing sometimes, it was better than wondering what to talk about. Joe dropped him off and told him where to go to get a lift for the next stage of his journey. They said their goodbyes. Finton counted the money Stan had given to him, Jesus, Mary and Joseph, he exclaimed, twenty pounds, twenty bloody pounds, he was rich, he's never seen twenty pounds in his life, his eyes filled with tears. He wanted to cry, "Oh, Stan, your a saint." he cried to himself. So now he had over thirty pounds, he would do what Stan said and keep it safe and try to make it last for a very long time. He would give some to Aunty Mary and Uncle Paddy and put the rest away some where safe.

When he reached Manchester it didn't take long for him to get another lift to Bridgevale from a farmer, he had taken a lorry load of cattle to the port and was on his way back home. They each had a problem with each other's accents and had to laugh out loud. "You're bound to find the Derbyshire accent worse than mine," he said, "and with yours it should be a right how do yer do." Finton was trying to work out what he had said, but couldn't. He then went on to tell the driver about his first meeting with Stand and Winnie, they being Scousers, he remembered how Winnie had sent him for a bath. How he had reeked of vomit, what a sight he must have looked, Winnie had said he smelt like a dead rat. They had had some good times and he would miss them very much. The driver waved him good-bye and gave him instructions on how to get to Bridgevale.

By the time he arrived, it was quite dark, he had been on the road for about twelve hours, there had been lots of walking with his thumb out and each lift had been welcome and the drivers glad of the company and a good chat, but by the time he had arrived at his destination the thoughts of telling anyone else about his boat trip over from Ireland made him bloody well want to scream.

He couldn't see very much but what he could see seemed to be a bit bleak, tall buildings and high chimney stacks and an acrid smell was coming from the foundry. I should have stayed in Bootle, he thought, he was missing the sea air already, the sea air and the scream of the seagulls. Anyway it might be different in the daylight, he would wait and see. He asked a man he met on the street the way to Uncle Paddy's railway terrace, he followed the instructions as best he could, what had the man said, first left, second right, then after that go up the road a bit and then the first street on the left. That lorry driver had been right about the accent, what a bloody palaver. After a while he arrived at Railway Terrace, it was very small but as neat as a new pin, Paddy and Mary made him very welcome, he could see that they were quiet poor. Everything they had was torn but clean and bright, when Finton handed them the two crisp five pound notes their eyes stood out like organ stops. "Bloody hell," said Paddy, "where the hell did you get that sort of money, Finton O'Grady. It's alreet, Uncle Paddy, I worked in the pub for Stan and Winnie and Stan gave me twenty pounds when I left. I also saved a bit myself." "Well, well, well." said Paddy, "They must have thought a lot about you lad, that they must to be sure an all."

They were very happy with the money and laid in bed that night and thanked God for the arrival of young Finton, the ten pounds would enable them to do many things that they had only dreams about, like a new bed for the two eldest lads, Sean and Patrick and warmer bedcovers for Liam and Mark. Yes, indeed it was a very happy Christmas they would be having this year. The money would not be squandered, however, most of it would be put aside and used sensibly. "You shall have a new warm coat, Mary." said Paddy "That you shall." and he would not be put off. She would have one and that was that. Mary's small work worn face was a picture, a new warm coat that would indeed be something she couldn't ever remember having a new coat, only hand me downs. This was bliss, "Sweet heaven, did we kiss the blarney stone,

Paddy?" she said "I feel like I have." "No, no," said Paddy, "It's the little people who have been watching us, the blarney stone just gives you the gift of the gab, so it does." Whoever it was, God bless them and Finton." said Mary. "Something has sent Finton to us for a reason,. I feel it in my bones, Paddy, I do." "Well, we will see, Mary, time will tell, go to sleep, we've an early start tomorrow."

Finton slept in the front parlour. Mary had made him a bed up in the corner of the room, it was a fold-up bed and would be stored under the stairs in the daytime. It was quite comfy, but very noisy, every time he moved the springs made a hell of a din, so he tried to be as quiet as he could. The four boys were very nice and well behaved and they had asked him to go fishing with them tomorrow along the canal. He was looking forward to this and slept well after his long journey.

Saturday morning they were all up early, Finton could here them all moving about. He quickly got dressed, he still felt really tired, he could have slept for a week. "Top of the mornin', Finton," they said in turn, the boys laughed at their father, they only heard Irish spoken at home and it was funny to hear some of the sayings Paddy came out with. There was oatmeal for breakfast and plenty of milk, Paddy had been to the farm early that morning. Also a slice of fresh toast each done on the open fire, the smell of fresh toast was always sure to make anyone drool, with butter and jam, a kings feast, they were sure. When they were all full they went to get the fishing rods and baskets and off they went. This was Finton's first glimpse of the town, it doesn't look too bad, lots of rows of houses, all neat and tidy with the steps all scrubbed and finished off with donkey stone. Sean gave this information to Finton who wondered what it was. Plenty of window boxes but without flowers because of the frost. Finton found it very cold and was glad of the scarf and gloves lent to him by Paddy.

He could see the mill where he would start work on the Monday morning, 20th December. It was a very large building, he'd never seen anything so large before and his guts started to churn at the thought of walking into the place. "You'll like it at the shed," remarked Patrick, "It smells very nice, I'm going to work there when I leave school." Up the high street they walked, there were lots of people shopping and there was a market too. He was amazed that anyone could stand there in the cold, it was freezing. The canal wasn't very far away and they walked for a while until they were away from the barges with all there noise. It would have to be quiet before the fish would bite. They sat down and for two freezing hours they caught nothing. Finton was sure that there were no fish in the canal. He decided that he couldn't stand the cold any longer, "have you lot had enough yet?" he pleaded, "I'm frozen." They didn't really want to go, but Finton was blue with cold so they reluctantly folded up their tackle and threw the remaining worms into the water as they walked along. Finton began to feel a little warmer, the exercise was good for his circulation which he had felt had stopped for ever.

Aunty Mary had dinner simmering on the hob when they returned and the aroma was unbelievable. They were all starving but Mary said it wouldn't be ready until twelve o'clock, so they took Finton round the rest of the town until he had seen most of it. The hills looked good for walkers he decided and intended to walk on them as soon as was possible. On their return dinner was ready, stew and dumplings with lots of thick slices of fresh baked bread and a big mug of steaming tea. This was the life, I can put up with this thought Finton. After dinner all he wanted to do was to sleep and Mary seeing his eyes closing packed him off to the front room. "Have a lie down on the settle." she told him. It was hard and uncomfortable but he slept like a baby, full to the brim with stew and dumplings.

The rest of the family crept about, they knew that without the money he had bought them they wouldn't have been eating stew and dumplings today it would have been something not so appetising. They all agreed that Finton was a grand lad and were glad that he would be living with them. "He's nothing like our Declan or his mother, Eileen, he must take after our grandparents, still he's a broth of a boy, to be sure." Paddy said

When Finton awoke, he wondered where he was, it was pitch black. He waited until his eyes had become accustomed to the darkness, then he made his way stealthily towards the chink of light he could see at the bottom of the door. He'd slept for four hour he couldn't believe it, "Sorry Aunty, I didn't mean to sleep so long can I help with anything?" "You just sit down, my lad, get your strength up ready for the shed, you'll need it." They talked about Ireland and of his parents and friends they hadn't seen for years. It was nice to talk and Mary felt a longing to go back over the water but knew they couldn't afford it. I haven't been back in over twenty five years, Finton. I sometimes think I never will, I was fifteen when I came to England and I can't see me ever going back. I got married late on to Paddy and now I've got four boys and I'm forty, a bit old for a mother but I love them all very much. "You'll never be old, Aunty Mary." he said, feeling sorry for the poor soul. He remembered his mother saying of Mary, she's as plain as a pike staff, don't think anyone will ever marry her but Paddy came along and they were amazed when she wrote and told them of her marriage and subsequent four children. She made a very good wife and mother and they were all very happy. Paddy was ten years older than her and he had always worked very hard, in fact he looked very much older and many thought the boys were his grandchildren. Still it was nothing to do with anyone else, so that was that, said Mary.

The first day at the shed was upon him and there was no turning back, he walked there alone and found his way to where he started his job. Cyril Lomas was waiting for him, showed him what he was supposed to do. Finton's head was spinning, how the hell would be ever be able to do all the things expected of him. When he went through the doors into the weaving shed for the first time he was struck dumb. So much noise, so many women. He kept his head down and walked into the big metal post, everyone was watching him and they all fell about laughing. It was on the first day that he caught sight of Cameo Moore. She was like an angel the most beautiful girl he had ever seen. He would get to know her that was for sure and get to know her well.

CHAPTER

11

So it was that he waited for her on the morning of New Years' Eve, hoping she would be able to attend the dance, then he would be able to hold her close and look into her beautiful eyes, he would walk her home and maybe, just maybe he would get to kiss her goodnight. He made his way to where she worked her looms. They were standing idle, she wasn't there, maybe she had gone to look for him, he rushed back as fast as he could, no Cameo was to be seen, so he went back again, still she wasn't there. Bessie was watching him, she beckoned him over, she shouted something at him, but he couldn't hear or understand what she said, he was looking at her hopelessly, then Fanny came along, "She's trying to tell you the lass hasn't come in today," "Oh," he said trying to make out he wasn't interested, "is that a fact." he answered. He walked away deeply disappointed, where was she would she be in later on today, he spent all day long up and down the shed trying not to look for her. A large plain woman was weaving her looms, Mr. Entwhistle didn't like them to remain idle for long. There was money to be made.

All Finton could do was wait for the night time and hope that she would be at the dance. What would he do if she wasn't there? No, he wouldn't think about it, he couldn't. That night he couldn't eat his meal, Aunty Mary was fussing, "I'm not hungry." he said. "I had a lot to eat at work today. One of the ladies gave me buns. She thinks I need feeding up." "The cheek of the devil," Mary said, "Does she think I starve you to death." "Oh, Aunty Mary, don't get mad, she means well." He had to pacify her for ages and he wished he hadn't opened his mouth.

He was dressed and out at last, he couldn't wait to see Cameo, he almost ran to the dance hall, it hadn't started yet, so he hung around hoping he would meet her. It was very cold and he wished he was wearing his overcoat but he couldn't wear it with his best suit, it was brown and looked terrible with his dark blue suit and black shoes. So he would have to put up with the cold, he had never known cold like it in his life and he sometimes wished for home, until he thought of Cameo and then he wouldn't have been anywhere else in the world. "AT' comin' in owt o' cold," he almost jumped out of his skin. It was Les from work, he was with a couple of mates, "Oh alreet," said Finton and followed them in like a sop, he would have liked to stay and look out a bit longer, but he would watch the door and that way he would be the first to see her. Well he kept his vigil all night, he was pestered by dozens of girls and he was feeling pretty pissed off with trying to be polite and smile all the time. He made his tenth trip to the bar and by that time he was feeling rather the worse for wear. It made him feel rather belligerent too, she's not bloody well going to turn up, he knew it was late and people were getting ready to go home, he spotted one of the local girls making her way towards him. She wanted the last dance and no way would he be dancing with her again, he turned quickly and went to the gent's toilet and he stayed there until the waltz was well under way, then he slipped out as quickly as he could, trying not to be noticed.

He felt like going to her house and banging on the door calling her a bitch, but he knew he never would. Perhaps her mam was worse, she had said she was poorly. That would be it, she was a good girl, he could tell she wasn't one to leave her sick mother to go out enjoying herself. He had to think this to keep himself from going mad, he wanted to see her so bad. He got home and quickly went to bed. He could dream about her no one could stop him from doing that and tomorrow we would find her somehow, he had to.

Camy slept fitfully that night and was up early the next day. She wished the kids a happy New Year and asked Joe to go up stairs and see if mam wanted a cup of tea and some breakfast. She made up the fire and put on the porridge pan, it was always the same, she wondered what they would eat if there was no porridge oats in the world. Joe came back down and told her mam would have a cup of tea but nothing to eat. mam never seemed to eat these days, she would have a word with Aunty Ada, maybe she could get her to eat.

After breakfast she washed up the dishes, Lizzie helped her and together everything was done for when Aunty Ada came round. They would have their meal together , like that first Christmas mam was poorly, it had been really nice and perhaps she would be able to get away for a walk and look around for Finton. Unless he had met someone else last night, she hoped with all her heart that he hadn't.

Aunty Ada turned up with Uncle Ted and she was pleased that Camy had prepared the veg., so the meat was put into the oven and Aunty Ada busied herself, while Ted read the morning paper, "He's still mytherin' about that Chamberlain," Aunty Ada shouted to Camy. "If I were in parliament he'd still bloody worry." she said Camy told Aunty Ada about her mam's poor appetite, "I'll see to that, lass. She's got to get her strength back, we'll have to make her small tasty things that will do her good." Ada was worried, she knew Sal wasn't picking up like she should be. Her eyes filled with tears, she wouldn't give up without a fight. By God, I'll make her eat, by God I will, she vowed. "Has he got up yet?" she asked, "No Aunty Ada, not yet." "I'll see her when he's shifted his bloody carcass." she said to Camy, they both felt the same way about Jim Moore.

After they had eaten and the washing up had been done, Camy was allowed to go out but she had to take the kids with her, so off they trooped, "lets walk down to the canal." said Alex, "Maybe we will see the ducks, our Camy." "Right then we will." she said, but the ducks were nowhere to be seen, the canal was freezing over and soon everyone would be trying to slide on it. It was a very dangerous game but they wouldn't be told. Someone shouted to Camy, it was Aggie, "Bye eke Aggie," said Camy "I haven't seen thee fer ages, where'st been keepin yerself." "Oh me mam has been goin' to other places, so we haven't been round 'er fer months now. Ow's that lad of yours?" enquired Camy. "OH, I hate 'im," said Aggie, "he were two timin' me wi me sister, the bloody rat." "What a shame, Aggie I'm right sorry." said Camy. "Oh, don't be, there's plenty more fish in th' sea." said Aggie. Alex and Lizzie wanted to see inside the barge, so Aggie took them on board, they were gone for about ten minutes and their faces were all aglow on their return. "Can I live on one of these, our Camy?" asked Alex. "Can I?" said Lizzie, "it's great." She had to drag them away, "Come on, we came out for a walk, are you coming with us Aggie?" So Aggie walked along with them, she promised the kids they could go back on board the next day after Sunday School. Aggies' little brothers and sister would be playing with them. "Have yer got a boyfriend yet Camy?" asked Aggie. Camy went bright red "Oh yer 'ave, come on Miss Cameo, tell us?" "I won't dunna be so daft." Aggie wouldn't be put off, I know that bloody daft look, so come on tell Aunty Aggie." "Well," said Camy "There is someone I really like but I've not bin out wi im. He wanted me to go'th dance last night but they wouldn't let me out, me mam's poorly agin." "Couldn't yer sneak out? I would've." said Aggie, "They wouldn't keep me in, bugger that. So you stayed 'ome like a good girl an he probably had it wi' somebody else."

"What do yer mean 'ad it?" "Yer know," said Aggie "got it out an put it in somebody." She made very crude gestures, "I love it." she said, "I did it al't time wi' that rat." she laughed, "Oh, Aggie!" Camy was shocked, "You didna, honest?" "Course I bloody did," said Aggie, "it was nice, warm and nice, we used to do it every day, about two or three times a day. Thats the only thing I miss about the rat, he was doin it to me sister as well and she bloody liked it as well. Any road she's got bigger tits than me so he's her boyfriend now. I told me mam, but she wanna bothered, just told her not ter gin in't puddin' club, that's all." Camy was really shocked at their behaviour, she'd never really met anyone who admitted they actually did it. "Bloody Hell, Aggie. I canna believe it." "Ave you ever 'ad it?" she asked Camy. "No I 'aven't, me Dad would bloody kill me." she shuddered at the thought, "I'm not goin' to 'til I get married she said." Aggie laughed out loud, "You'll 'ave a bloody long wait then you ain't got a boyfriend, so what are you goin' ta do?" "I'll just keep waiting until Mr. Right comes along. "Mr., who?" Aggie wanted to know, so Camy explained to her. "Can't see much sense in it meself, but if that's what they wants, good luck ter yer girl, as me mam would say." By this time they had walked a couple of miles down the canal path so they turned back, Alex and Lizzie skipped happily along, unable to hear the conversation taking place. It was a good job too, they sometimes repeated things they had overheard to mam or Dad then all bloody hell broke loose. They said they would meet her tomorrow. "Why don't yer com'th Sunday School wi us?" said Camy. "No thanks," came the reply "I can't do wi Bible pushers." Camy wondered what they were but didn't want to look thick and stupid, so she just smiled and went on her way. They were almost at the end of the canal turn when she spotted Finton, he was sitting on the wall. She felt sick inside, Oh God, do I look a mess," she wondered, "is my nose clean and my teeth, have they got any dinner lodged in them. She was all of a fluster, but pretended to be calm and aloof. He doffed his cap at her, "Good Afternoon, Miss Cameo Moore," he said "Hello, Finton and how are you today." "Oh, I'm fine," he said, "the dance was grand last night. I didn't see you, did you go?" trying to pretend he hadn't noticed. "No, mam was poorly, I couldn't leave her on her own", she was trying to speak properly and it was hard, her posh voice as the kids called it.

"I'm sorry about that," said Finton "is there a chance you could get out another night?" She looked into his eyes, she felt giddy, what's up with me, she asked herself. "Well I can try. I'm going up to my sisters later on about seven o'clock, up market street. I can meet you if you want to." "I'll meet you." he said quickly, too quickly really, but he couldn't help himself. "Righto. I'd better get home, there's lots to be done." "Are these your family?" he asked. "Yes," replied Camy "this is Lizzie and Alex." they said "Hello," nice looking family they were, he thought to himself, very nice looking indeed. They waved good-bye to each other and she scuttled off home, God if anything stops me going to our Jean's tonight, I'm going to die. God, please be on my side, just this once. Aunty Ada didn't mind staying with Sal, so off Camy went just after seven o'clock, her heart was thumping so loud she was sure everyone she passed could hear it. Finton was waiting round the corner, he had got there early, he was so eager to see her. They looked at each other and both knew suddenly how they felt, the attraction for each other was so strong. Thank God it was so dark, thought Finton. He could feel the stirring in his loins. I've got a bloody great erection, he thought. Thank God for cold nights and long overcoats. He felt for her hand and she didn't resist, they walked in silence. They didn't really need to talk, they were so happy. When they were just round the corner from Jean's, she stopped, "I'll have to leave yu here, Finton," she said, "He pulled her to him and held her close. He couldn't believe the tumultuous feelings he had for her, it almost took his breath away. Gently he kissed her neck, then her cheek and began to seek her mouth, Camy had never been kissed before in her life and she was a little afraid, but her feelings for him were so strong that she trembled from head to foot and couldn't stop. His lips were on hers at last and he forced open her mouth but gently and flicked his tongue in and out. She almost passed out with the pleasure of it. She swayed, he held her tighter, she kissed him back it was the most wonderful experience of her entire life. She wanted it to go on forever. They stayed like that for over half an hour and finally she had to prize herself away from him. I'll have to go Finton, I really must." "Can I see you home afterwards?" he asked. "No, I'm sorry, my brother in law always insists on walking home with me." He was downcast, but urged her to meet him the following night. "I'll try Finton, I really will." they kissed once more, then he watched her go inside her sisters house, and he wanted to shout 'hooray' and dance on the rooftops.

Jean was pleased to see her, she was knitting baby clothes. She wanted to know about mam, she was worried that she wasn't getting any better, "Aunty Ada will sort her out Jean, don't worry." "No yer canna do worrying about everybody," said Arthur, "you've got baby to think about, your mam will be alreet, she's tough as old boots, as't be wi a Dad like yours." They all laughed at this but deep down they were worried sick.

Sunday morning Camy took the kids to Sunday School, there was a lantern slide show and the three really enjoyed it, Camy read a story for all the little ones and then Miss Thomson played the piano and they all sang 'Jesus wants me for a sunbeam', it was time to go home for dinner. They were all hungry, it had been a long time since breakfast. Ada was waiting for them, everything was ready to dish up, Ada wouldn't stay because Jim was still about it wasn't time for the pubs to open yet. So she went home and left Camy to dish out the dinner. She couldn't eat herself, she wanted to think about Finton, so she just nibbled and was lost in thought when she felt a whack round her ear. "Bleedin hell, what was that?" Jim was at the back of her, don't you bloody well ignore we lady," he shouted. "I'm sorry Dad, I didn't hear you." she almost crawled under the table with fear, "I said take your mam her friggin dinner." She jumped up right away "OK Dad, sorry." she said again. He wasn't interested in what she had to say, "Shut your bastard mouth and get on wi' it." he roared and them he sat down to eat his food. Joe, Teddy, Lizzie and Alex sat frozen at the table, not daring to look up from their plates, afraid they might drop a spud or slurp, if they did they knew what to expect. Camy had laid a tray for her mam and made up a plate of the nicest titbits she could find. She knew her mam wouldn't eat much of it but she had to try. Sal was sat up in bed, she was wearing Ada's bed jacket it was pink angora wool and she looked lovely in it apart from her pallor, she always looked nice her mam.

"Here you are mam," she said trying not to show the tears she had just wiped away. Sal looked up at her "What's matter Camy, have yer bin weepin', ey?" "Oh, it's now't mam," Sal could see the red mark up her face and neck, "has yer Dad done that then," "Aye," said Camy "I didn't hear him saying summat to me, I was thinkin'." Sal could see she was hurt and upset, "Well yer know yer Dad, yer know what he's like, keep out of his bloody way and yer wunna get 'urt, it's yer own daft fault." It's a good job I didn't want any bloody sympathy. thought Camy, 'Cause I dunna get any, a bloody dog gets more than me. When I marry Finton I'll leave this lot and bugger off to Ireland, that thought cheered her up no end. "Aunty Ada's made a syrup sponge pudding and custard, mam are yer goin' ter have a little taste. No Camy, there's plenty to get down me here. I can't manage a puddin' as well. Will yer get me a nice cup of tea, later on?"

Camy heard the back door slam, thank God he's gone out, peace, bloody peace, she said to herself. Later on she told Aunty Ada she was going to see Nellie and Aunty Ada said not to be late.

I've escaped from the prison again, she said under her breath. No it's not a prison really, I mustner think like that, I love mam and the kids, it's just Dad, he's so horrible. I wish he were dead. Rounding the corner of the street she saw Finton waiting for her. Every time she saw him she felt sick to the pit of her stomach, with joy of course, "Hello Finton." she greeted him, "Hello Miss Cameo Moore," he said pretending to bow to her and doffing his cap. "You are a silly bugger Finton, behave yourself," she chastised him. "I can't help it Cameo," he replied "you make me feel so happy."

They walked through the town quickly and down towards the canal, there in the dark, they held each others hand. No one could see them now. He chatted on and she was happy just to listen to his lilting Irish brogue. After a while, he stopped and pulled her to him. He kissed her eagerly and hungrily she kissed him back. She hadn't had much practice but he was so easy to kiss, he made it feel so wonderful. His kisses grew stronger and more passionate and she thought she would faint away with the ecstasy of it. His tongue flicked in and out of her mouth and she wanted to die there and then with him with his kisses. Then she felt his hand begin to slide over her breast, she was powerless to stop him, he groaned deeply. "Oh, Cameo," he whispered, "Cameo." Her nipples stood out and he pinched them between his fingers, he opened her coat a little more and slid his hand inside her blouse where he continued to stroke her firm ripe breasts. Before she knew it he was bending down and had her nipple in his mouth. She felt a charge like an electric shock run down her spine. "Finton stop, please stop." She knew this was wrong, she shouldn't be doing this but it was absolutely wonderful and she wanted it to go on forever. But Finton heard her cry out and he stopped. "Cameo, I'm sorry, do forgive me," he begged her I've lost her now, he thought, how could I got this far so soon what a bloody fool I am. He straightened her clothes and hugged her close, "say you'll forgive me, Cameo." he begged her. "Tell me," "Oh, Finton, it's alreet it's just that I think it's wrong," she couldn't go on, so she pulled his face down to her's and kissed him with all the feeling she could muster.

"Cameo," he said, "I want to say something to you and I don't want you to laugh at me," he looked her in the eye and he was deadly serious, "I fell in love with you the first time I saw you, I love you with all my heart and with all my soul, I will never ever love anyone else until my dying day. Please tell me you feel the same or I'll jump in the canal and drown myself." "Oh, Finton, I love you too, so very much. All I can think about is you. I can't eat or sleep properly because of my love for you, don't ever leave me, please don't. She felt like crying, tears were in her eyes. "Right said Finton, "So therefore we will get married someday in the future when I have saved enough money." They both agreed and they hugged and kissed each other. Then he told he had wanted to make love to her but he would wait until things were better. "You will have to keep pushing me off," he laughed, 'because I want to all the time, I can't help it, I'm only human."

Camy told him she didn't know how, so he would have to teach her. "I daren't ever get pregnant," she told him about her Dad and what he would do, she told him of Jim's cruelty and Finton wanted to kill him with his bare hands. She talked of her mam and how she wasn't getting any better. "I'd like to meet your mam," he said, "I bet you look like her." Camy didn't tell him her mam never hugged or kissed them, never showed any love or care, he probably wouldn't understand. He spoke about his parents in Balynahinch and of his life there, it sounded wonderful, "how could you bear to leave it?" she asked. "There was little work so I came here, my family is very poor," he said, he didn't mention the farmers' wife or the shot gun. She must never know about that episode in his life. He would love her and care for her all the days of her life, as soon as was possible. "Cameo Moore, You'll be Mrs. Cameo O'Grady one day, that's for sure and he meant every word.

CHAPTER

12

They continued to meet whenever they possibly could always hungry for each other. The weeks dragged in to months and soon Jean gave birth to her baby girl on the 14th June, 1938. She would be christened Elizabeth Jean, Lizzie was very pleased about that. They've called her after me she told everyone.

Camy decided it was time the family met Finton, so she went round to Aunty Ada's and asked her what she must do. "Well I'm right pleased for thee lass," she said and Uncle Ted was too. Your mam's a bit better now so it won't upset her. Bring him round tomorrow night after thee Dad's gone out and me and Uncle Ted will be there and we can all have a good look at this handsome Irish lad of your's.

Ada had known about Finton via the local gossips for some time so it was no surprise. Anyway Camy was a woman now and a little beauty. She deserved a better life than the drudge she was at home. Ada knew that when Camy left the family she would have to do more for Sal and the others. Mary could help too and Jean, they would be alreet the lass deserved a break. So it was she told Finton and he dressed in his best, arrived just after eight o'clock when Jim had gone to the pub. Camy went to bring him in from the corner of the street, he said "Hello" to the kids then Camy ushered him through to the parlour where mam, Ada and Ted were waiting. She held his hand tightly and said "mam, Aunty Ada, Uncle Ted, this is Finton," he wafted into the room and all eyes were upon him. By eck, thought Ada, he was a strikingly handsome young lad. Ted got up to shake his hand. Sal stared at him is disbelief, no, it couldn't be, it wasn't, it is "William," she said. They all looked round at her, she tried to get up off the settle. What the ecks up with her, they all thought. Finton, smiled at her, "Finton O'Grady, Mrs. Moore." he said. Her eyes rolled in her head and she clutched at her chest and started to gasp, they all fell about in panic. "Ted, get her tablets," "Camy, get water, quick. They were running around in circles. Sal had passed out and they all thought that she was dead. Ada asked Finton to run to the doctors house and tell him to come out, quick. This he did, what did I say, he thought. What's wrong with the woman. She looked as though she had seen a ghost. Before long doctor Hallam had arrived. Camy put the kids to bed, Finton had been sent home. He was in a daze, what a night!

Sal could not be moved, she had suffered a massive heart attack. He didn't know if she would pull through. We will just have to take one day at a time if she lasts the night then there was a small chance, but he couldn't be sure.

Ada was beside herself, "I can't loose our Sal, Ted, I can't. I love her so much." Ted tried to comfort his wife, she wouldn't go home, they all sat round Sal in the parlour. Ada sent Camy off to bed, "You've got work in't morning lass, so get thee sen a few 'ours sleep, we'll not be leavin' her."

When Jim Moore came home he was stricken by the inert form of his wife on the settle and the haunted look on the faces of Ada and Ted. "What's up wi Sal?" he asked, they told him as much as they could, "I'll stay up wi her Ada." You and Ted get some sleep, but Ada wouldn't go, "No, I'm staying err, Jim Moore and nowt'll shift me." So they all sat watching over Sal, praying she would recover.

Camy was in a daze, what was wrong with mam, why had she called Finton, William. She had looked so stricken. Her face she couldn't describe the look on her mother's face. Would she die, "Please, God, don't let mam die." However would they live without her, she was mam and Camy loved her so much. In the early hours of the morning, Sal rallied round, Ada rushed to her side, "Sal, are yer alreet lass, whatever come over you?" Sal whispered low to her sister, "Ada do something for me, please I beg of you." "Anything Sal, just tell me what," "Write to the Brannigans at Fallows End, you remember," "What's she saying." said Jim. "It's alreet Jim, just let her walk to me awhile," Sal continued when Jim sat down again. "Write and ask them about William, ask them where William is now." She drifted back to sleep. Ada walked over to Ted, "Come on we've gotta get home awhile," she said "Jim, you sit with Sal and we'll be back in two ticks, if she gets worse, come for me right." Jim agreed to this, so they set of back to Ada's.

"What the bloody Hell was all that about, our Ada," asked Ted, bewildered, "I'm as wise as you Ted, Sal asked me to write to them Brannigans at Big 'ouse in London, summat to do with a man called William, it's got to do wi when she left London looking like bloody death warmed up. Oh,

Ted." she cried, "She's goin ter die, I know she is," wailed Ada. "Now, now lass, calm down, she's rallied round before, she's tough as old boots, you mark my words." Ada got out the writing paper and envelopes and Ted was sent to look for Sal's old letters from the big house which Ada kept upstairs in a big tin box. Ada wasn't much of a letter writer but she had to do it she had promised Sal on what might be her death bed. Her body shook with sobs, Ted rushed downstairs with the letters. "Come on Ada, bear up lass, this wunna get they anywhere." After a while Ada composed herself and began to write asking the Brannigans the whereabouts of someone named William that her sister had known at Fallows End. She explained that Sally was very ill and might not live and urged them if possible to answer by return of post. She copied the address from Sal's old letters and it was ready for Ted to post first thing that morning.

They then returned to Sal's house to sit out the remainder of the night. Jim was wandering about like a man possessed, wringing his hands, he had to talk, Ada he pleaded, I've got to talk to you. I know you hate me, I know I've bin a right bastard wi Sal but I've bin driven to it, you dunna know everythin." What on earth at thee talkin about man?" asked Ada.

So Ted sat with Sal and Ada stalked in to Jim in the kitchen "Now, lets be knowin' what's bin wrong then Jim Moore." He then told her everything Sal had told him all those years ago when he had finished, Ada was completely struck dumb. Sal, she thought to do somethin like this and never let on. "Say somethin' Ada for God's sake, say somethin'." Ada spluttered

"Jim, I dunna know what to say. I can 'ardly believe it. Our Sal, 'avin' an affair wi' Master William, son and heir, him killin' his self an er lossin' her baby. Then she marries you co's she's expectin', our Jim, and you say she's never loved thee." "No," he said, "but I've alus loved er, I've bin a rotter wi' er because she would never show any love for me. I alus hoped one day, she would learn ter care for me, the more she shoved me away the worse I treated er. I'm sorry Ada I just wanted her to love me the way she loved that bloody William, but she never did.

Ada saw Jim in a different light that morning. She could tell he was telling the truth and she felt right sorry for the man, something she never thought she would hear herself say, poor Jim, what a bloody awful life. She didn't however tell him about the letter, best just to send it. The man was dead but Sal wouldn't believe it until confirmation arrived, if it ever did. Perhaps she was having hallucinations. She had looked at Finton and thought he was this William fellow. Doctor Hallam called round to see

Sal early that morning when everyone was getting ready for work and school. He listened to her heart, felt her pulse, gave her a small capsule with water and left some more for the pain. "I'm not very happy with her," he told Ada, Ted and Jim, "she's getting weaker, I'd send her to the hospital but moving her could prove fatal. Keep her quiet and still, don't force her to eat but drinks if she could manage them. I'll be calling back this afternoon." he bade them good morning and left. They all felt worse after that, he hadn't given them very much hope. Ada went about quietly weeping, Jim did the same. Ted said he didn't know if he was on his arse or his elbow, God Almighty was all he could say when Ada told him the story of Sal and William Brannigan.

He'd posted the letter after he had walked Camy to work that morning, "Yer best at work lass, it'll take thee mind off things. Camy wanted to stay with her mam but she also wanted to see Finton, poor lamb, he must be worried to death. Bet he hadn't slept all night, like herself. She would have to tell Mary and Ted would call on all the others, so they could see their mother, perhaps for the last time. A cold shiver went down her spine. Finton was waiting for her just inside the mill, he was white with worry. She told him mam had had a massive heart attack. She didn't know why she had called him William. "I think she were seeing things Finton, dunna blame yerself, please. I'll see thee later on" She worked all day in a dream, she even smiled at Frank Wright who she hated with a vengeance because she didn't know who he was her mind was in such turmoil.

Ada was the same, she went over all the happenings, she still couldn't believe Sal would keep such secrets from her for all these years. She took a bowl of warm water and a flannel and washed Sal's hands and face jus to freshen her up. Sal was clutching the cameo brooch so tightly, Ada wondered what on earth it was. She wouldn't let it go, so Ada wiped round it. She was in pain so Ada gave her one of the capsules with a drop of water, they worked very quickly and she settled back to sleep again. She wouldn't let go of that silly cameo brooch, she said to Jim. You don't know about that Ada. William gave it to her and she keeps it next to her heart always. She even called Camy after it, that's why I give Camy such a hard time, jealousy I think. I give that poor bloody girl hell because of a friggin brooch, she knows nowt about, he dissolved into a flood of tears and Ada wanted to hug him to her ample breasts. Oh, Jim, what could she say, the man must have suffered so badly all these years. They had called him all the names under the sun all these years not knowing what was going on. I'll never understand anyone ever again, thought Ada. That afternoon and evening the family called round to see their mam. Jim and

Tilly with Sally Victoria, Harry and Peggy, Jean and Arthur with baby Elizabeth and Mary and Brian. The youngsters were taken round to Ada's after school, so Sal could have plenty of peace and quiet.

Young Jim and Harry were wringing their hands in despair, it's his bloody fault they both agreed, he would get a bloody good hiding off them both as soon as he set foot through the door. Ada butted in with her pennyworth, she told them a little bit about the events of the previous night and told them to lay off their father, they didn't know it all the circumstances. "By heck, Aunty Ada, I never thought I'd see the day you took his side against us." said Jim. "I'm not taking sides you two, so listen to me and behave yourselves or else, I'll tell thee the rest when I'm up to it." They went home feeling robbed of the pleasure of giving Jim Moore a bloody good hiding. It was something they had promised themselves for years and if mam died, by hell, he was going to get it, the bastard would get his bloody come-uppence.

Six days after Sal's bad do there was a knock at the front door, Ada looked through the window, "Ted," she called "There a bloody great big car outside, what'll I do?" Ted peered through the lace curtains, "There's one of them chauffeurs wi' it." he answered. He answered the door, Ada wouldn't go.

On the doorstep stood a very plump woman about forty years, she was dressed in the most beautiful clothes Ted had ever seen. He stood open mouthed, gawping at her, "Good-day Sir," she said. "I'm hear to see Sally Smith." "Oh, sorry," said Ted, "come in," "I'm Mrs. Ernestini Lawson-Groves." she added. Ted didn't know what to say, she was so posh he darn't open his mouth. He ushered her into the parlour where Ada was waiting. "It's Mrs. Ernestini Lawson-Groves," she said, "are you Sally's sister Ada?" "That's right," said Ada trying to speak properly, it was difficult under the circumstances. Ernestini walked over to the settle where Sal lay, white and still, "is she alive," she asked "Oh, aye", said Ada, "she's still very poorly though, we didna' expect yer to come out err from London," she added. "It was the least I could do, when I found out what had happened." They sat her down and made her a cup of tea . She looked round at the clean but shabby room not at all what she was used to, but they were decent people, hard working and honest, she could tell that and they clearly loved Sally very much. Ada told her the story that Jim had told them and waited while she composed herself.

At that moment Sal opened her eyes and looked at them one by one. "Miss Ernestini," she whispered "you came, I've been praying you would sen word of William," Ernestini moved her chair to sit closer to Sally,

"How are you, Sally, it's good to see you after all these years." she had seen lots of dying people in her time and Sally wasn't here for very long that she knew from the look of her. "Sally, I want to completely honest with you. Can you take what I have to tell you, you've got to be very strong to hear what I have called to tell you." Sal nodded her head "Please tell me everything. I know William is still alive, I've seen his son ." Ada and Ted looked at each other, she's gone barmy, poor lass Ada's look said to her husband. "After I had received your letter, I set out to find out the truth about what had happened, my parents both died some years ago and I was away staying with friends when my brother died." "You're wrong," said Sally, "he's not dead, I tell you." "Sally listen to me hear me out. First of all" said Ernestini, trying to keep Sally calm, "My brother William shot himself over a love affair. I didn't know it was with you, Sally. No one was allowed to tell me. My parents were beside themselves with grief. It was a truly awful time. After your letter" she added "I went through all my families letters and correspondence and I came across details of his love for you and how he couldn't live without you. My parents were sending him away to America and he couldn't go on without the woman he loved," she stopped to compose herself once again. "My parents did you the most terrible wrong Sally and I am so very sorry. I can never make up the wrong they did to you." her face was stricken, she couldn't go on. Tell me pleaded Sal, what wrong. "Well," continued Ernestini, "after you had fallen down the staircase on hearing of William's death, they had you taken to a private clinic. They thought you would die but you didn't, you gave birth to a son." "Yes, I know." said Sal, he died, my son died. "No, he didn't," whispered Ernestini, "he didn't die Sally, he lived. My parents paid the Matron to find him a home, they paid handsomely for her promise of confidentiality." Before Sally could interrupt her again, she went on. "I found the Matron and made her tell me the truth about the child, I threatened her with the law unless she told all. The baby was given to a childless couple who were never told of his parentage, that couple lived in Ballymahinch, Northern Ireland, the Child was called Finton O'Grady." A gasp went round the room. Sally groaned and passed out, the other dashed about fearing she had died. Finton, so that was why she had called ,William, he was probably very much like his father. "Ted" screamed Ada suddenly ,"Ted, Camy's in love with Finton." "Oh, bloody hell, Oh God, Ted, what are we going to tell her. She loves the lad with all her heart." Ada wept bitterly, was there no end to this, what was to become of Sal and Camy and poor Finton. What would Jim say about it all.

Ada told Ernestini about Camy and Finton, Ernestini was very concerned, what a terrible time they were having, she was sorry to bring them this awful news. Her parents had a lot to answer for and for the first time since their death, she was glad that they were no longer alive. They had been responsible for some terrible things. Her brother had a son, her a nephew and she had been deprived of him for twenty-five years. He also had been deprived of his inheritance, which was vast. He could have enjoyed so much, but she intended to make that up to him as soon as was possible.

She then informed Ada she would be staying at the best hotel in town and would they make it known to Finton that she, his aunty would be waiting to see him. She shook their hands and said for the tenth time, she was sorry about the unhappiness bought about by her parents and headed for her Rolls Royce car.

Everyone in the street was out gawping at it "Who's the bloody greet car owt side Moore's. What goin on ast King cum fer tea?" asked one young lad. Ernestini looked down her nose as they all gathered round her, her chauffeur opened the door for her made sure she was comfortable, doffed his smart uniform hat at Ada and Ted and drove off slowly towards the town.

When she had gone Jim returned, having heard on route about the posh lady and car on his way back through the town. He had been to get more pills for Sal from the pharmacy and had stopped for a couple of large brandies which he badly needed after the last few days. Everyone asked about Sal and sent their best regards. When Ada told him about Ernestini she expected him to loose his temper, but he didn't, he listened to her talk about William and her baby son and of the fact that the son was none other than Camy's boyfriend, Finton O'Grady even Jim Moore was stunned at this, he had seen the young man and had liked him. He knew Camy was courting him but never let on. He had played cards with him one night when he had first come to Bridgevale. The lad only knew him as Jim, so wouldn't know he was Camy's Dad, and now he learned that he was Sal's son, her first born of William Brannigan. How would she take it she hadn't come round properly yet. She did rally round a while later when Doctor Hallam called round again.

His face was very grim. "She hasn't got very long to live," he said, "I'm sorry, she is very week. There is nothing else I can do, if there was I would gladly do it." When he had gone they all wept together, don't let her see us crying, lets try to be cheerful asked Ada of them all. The whole family was sent for and Camy was told to bring Finton home with her.

They were all ushered in to see Sally, she was propped up on the settle, she looked really beautiful and no one could believe she was dying. Ada told Camy and Finton the story of Sally's' life in London about William, his death and about the son she had born. Camy was absolutely amazed her mam did all that and no one ever knew. Then Sally took over, said how sorry she was that she had never shown any love for them. She explained that she was afraid to love anyone ever again because she knew if she did they would surely be taken away from her. Camy cried, "I knew you loved me mam." She said. "I just knew it." Sally held Camy in her arms and kissed her tenderly. "I can say it now," she said. "I love you Camy, you have been such a good girl for me and now you have got to be stronger than ever because of what I have to tell you." Camy looked up at her mother, "Tell me?" She was puzzled, "What do ye mean, mam?" Sally beckoned Finton over and held his hand too, she stroked his face and a sob racked her whole body. She then told them the rest of the story at how Finton was indeed the son she had born to William Brannigan.

The impact came to them suddenly. They were brother and sister, no! no! no! Camy wanted to scream, but it stuck in her throat. Sally clutched their hands tightly. "My son," she said "My son, my Williams' son." she crossed her eyes and laid back, they looked at each other the pain was too great to bear. "Finton, Oh, Finton," whimpered Camy, he was so dazed he couldn't believe it. They sat for a while unable to come to terms with it all. It was then they realised that Sally wasn't breathing.

"Aunty Ada, Dad, someone." shouted Camy, Ada was there at Sal's side in seconds. She's gone she said, our Sal's gone, she slipped away peacefully. Everyone came into the room. Sally was dead no one could hurt her again and she had looked upon the face of her first born son, who she had thought was dead all those years. She had died happy there was a serene look on her face, almost a smile.

Camy and Finton were numb with shock, this couldn't be happening, mam was dead, their mother was dead, she was their mother not just hers, theirs. Finton couldn't grasp the situation at all, he was a simple Irish Catholic his Ma and Dada, who were they really. How could that dead woman be his mother, what about William Brannigan it was all too much for him.

He marched out of the house, Camy ran after him but he walked too quickly and she couldn't catch up with him, "Finton" she cried "Please don't go, come back Finton." But he did not acknowledge her at all. He must be feeling so mixed up, she couldn't take it in either. She went back to the house, the sound of weeping and body wrenching sobs filled the whole place. She wanted to scream at her mam, you can't die like this, it isn't fair woman, she looked round at them all from brother Jim down to little Alex and then Aunty Ada but the most grief stricken of all was her Dad, the sight of his heartbroken face twisted with pain was something she had never expected to see. Jim Moore weeping for his dead wife who would ever have thought it. She couldn't take her eyes off him. Well bloody well, why was he so upset, he didn't love her, he didn't love anyone only himself. The sight made her feel sick to her stomach. Someone was at the back door, she went to open it, it was Mrs. Lowe. She laid out the dead ready for the undertaker. She was a big strong capable woman. "Very sorry to hear yer bad news." she said to everyone and no one, she didn't look sorry she enjoyed her work, wouldn't change it for a gold clock Ada had always said. Everyone cleared out of the parlour so she could do whatever she did with a dead body. Mary and Jean were making endless cups of tea, no one thought to ask Camy how she felt, how she was coping with the terrible loss of her mam or finding out that the man she loved so desperately was her brother, born out of wedlock twenty-five years ago to a rich mans son and her mam. What would become of Finton and herself. She knew you couldn't marry your brother and Finton was that, she felt a sharp pain in her chest.

I'm going to die like me mam, she thought, my bloody hearts broke. She didn't care she wanted to die, she didn't want to live without her beloved Finton, she looked at her family and much as she loved them all, she loved Finton much, much more. Let me wake up and find this is all a bloody bad dream. mam would be here as always, Dad would be at the pub, the kids would be happy, she would be getting her cloths ready for work, everything would be like it was before.

Please God, let it be like it was before, she thought, it's got to be a dream, a nightmare, but it wasn't, it was all true, they were all weeping. Finton had run away. Who would look after the kids now that mam was dead, the bloody doormat, I'll bet, me that's who. I can't do that I've got to find Finton, we can run away together, where no one would know us. She would find Finton and tell him right away.

Quickly she slipped out of the house, she went round to Finton's Uncle Paddy's but he wasn't there. What's the matter, my girl?" asked Aunty Mary, seeing the wild look on Camy's face, "It's me mam, she's dead." said Camy, "Oh, I'm sorry, sure it's terrible it is, all those children and no mother to love them, she went on," Camy felt panic rise in her breast, she ran down the road where was he. After trying everywhere she knew, she went down to the canal to a spot they loved to spoon together. She wasn't afraid of the darkness tonight, nothing could hurt her more than she was hurting now. Let the spooks come out of the ground, let the devil himself jump over the wall and she would smack him a bugger. Nothing mattered anymore, nothing would ever be the same again.

Before she reached him, she heard his sobbing. She ran to him, Finton, I've been looking for you for hours, she pulled him to into her arms. "Oh, Cameo, my love, what are we going to do." Someone threw a bucket of water from one of the barges, it made them jump out of their skins. "I don't know, Finton, I just don't know. I only know I don't want to live without you. I can't live without you. I can't take over as mam to all the kids and be Dad's doormat, to get thumped from mornin' til night, to be without you and cry myself to sleep every night, I can't do it." she dissolved into floods of tears, "I don't want to live without mam if your not with me either, I canna go on Finton. What shall we do."

Finton thought about it for a while, his family had betrayed him, pretending to be his ma and dada, never telling him the truth. They could have told him that. Now he was Cameo's brother. He could never see her again, the love of his life. He would go back to Ballymahinch, he couldn't stay here, but go back to what. There was nothing for him there now, everything he loved in life was here, Cameo was his life, he couldn't imagine ever being without her. He had fallen in love with her the first time he had seen her weaving her looms at the shed. "Cameo, I can't live without you, my dearest love, would you be able to go on with your life if I were to go away for a while?" he asked. She clung to him desperately, "No Finton, I will die if you leave me, I mean it, I canna go on without you and your love. I really don't want to live anymore. I've had enough, the heart ache is just too much to bear." "Shall we die together?" he asked, she looked up at him, "Do you mean it, Finton or are you just saying it?" "I mean it, Cameo, I don't want to live without you, you don't want to live without me, so lets die together, that way, we will be together for all eternity." It sounded so wonderful, "Yes, Finton lets, lets jump in the cut, she took his hand. "No, no little one," he half laughed, not in there, somewhere a bit better, what about the river Goyt that flows past the shed that's deeper and faster we would be carried further down stream and maybe never found." Their minds were made up, they would never go home again, never see the faces of their beloved family ever again, but it was the only way. There was no other way out for them if there was, they would have taken it.

Camy thought about her brothers and sisters, little Alex, young Lizzie, babies Sally Victoria and Elizabeth Jean. She thought of the love she had for Aunty Ada and Uncle Ted everyone at the weaving shed. She would never see again. They walked back along the canal and found the workman's hut where Finton had seen the rope, it wasn't very thick but it looked strong. They made their way down to the river Goyt, up stream from the mill so that no one would see them and try to stop them. They kissed each other passionately and clung to one another. Finton told her of his deep love for her and his only regret was that they had never made proper love, the love they were saving for the day that they were going to get married.

Finton wrapped the rope round their waists, "Let me tie it ," Camy asked "She tied a weavers knot, "They say a weavers knot will never break, Finton," "Lets hope it doesn't Cameo." He asked her "Have you any regrets, do you still want to do it, Oh, yes." she replied. Her eyes were wild and sparkling, she was ready to face death with the love of her life. "We will be together always Finton in paradise." she said. They kissed once more, holding each other tight they then plunged into the cold deep fast flowing river.

It was Aggie who found them early that morning, she was sneaking back to the barge from the Tinker caravan. She had been staying all night. They were bobbing like corks in the weir. Camy's petticoat had caught on the frame of an old bike and it had held them there still bound together in death as they had been in life, the weavers' knot held fast.

Printed in the United Kingdom
by Lightning Source UK Ltd.
104184UKS00001BA/15

9 781845 490164